DETROIT COMBAT

DETROIT COMBAT

RANDY WAYNE
WHITE
WRITING AS CARL RAMM

OPEN ROAD

INTEGRATED MEDIA

NEW YORK

Cover design by Andy Ross

ISBN: 978-1-5040-3520-0

This edition published in 2016 by Open Road Integrated Media, Inc.
180 Maiden Lane
New York, NY 10038
www.openroadmedia.com

DETROIT COMBAT

ONE

"Take off your clothes," ordered the woman. "I can't make any decision as long as you have your pants on. You're here for a screen test, aren't you? Well, aren't you?"

James Hawker stood just inside the door a suite of offices on the eighteenth floor of an East Jefferson Avenue smogscraper in downtown Detroit. The woman sat at a bare desk in a nearly bare room. Behind her there was a window. Through the window he could see the steeple of the Mariner's Church and, by leaning to the left, the December bleakness of Lake St. Clair. The steeple looked very old, very delicate against the stalagmite gloom of the city beyond.

"Screen test?" repeated James Hawker. "Oh . . . yeah . . . right—a screen test. I would like to take off all my clothes and stand in front of a camera. Why else would I be here?"

In the center of the room a bank of Klieg lights and a video camera sat on tripods above an empty bed. Beyond the bed was a door. Hawker assumed the screen test the woman mentioned had to do with the making of a pornographic film. He also assumed the door led to more offices—offices he wanted to see.

"Well?" asked the woman.

"Well?" echoed Hawker.

"Well, take your god damn clothes off! The camera team is working in the back set, but they'll be breaking in about twenty minutes, and you'd damn well better be ready!"

At the desk, the woman held a Styrofoam coffee cup in one hand and a Virginia Slims cigarette in the other. She used a peanut can as an ashtray. The woman, in her late forties, had silver-blond hair cut boyishly short and owlish glasses. Hawker wondered why anyone would try so hard to look like Geraldine Ferraro.

He had followed a pock-faced man and a woman into the skyscraper, then lost them in the crowded halls. He suspected the woman to be Brenda Jacobsen Paulie. He had recognized her from the photographs in his Detroit Kidnap Victims file. In the photographs she had wheat-colored hair and a very pretty face. They had dyed her hair inky black, and her eyes were bleary with drugs and lack of sleep, but Hawker was almost sure it was the same woman.

The man was either her keeper or her kidnapper, and they were somewhere in this building—maybe in this suite of offices.

Hawker had to find out.

Brenda Paulie was only one of at least thirteen women who had been kidnapped in the last twelve months. Paulie's story was as tragic as any of them. Only twenty-four years old, she had just graduated from law school. In June she married Blake

4

Paulie, a successful Detroit attorney. On the morning of September fifteenth, a Tuesday, the Paulies learned they were to be parents. Brenda was pregnant. They planned a celebration dinner for that evening.

The dinner was never to be.

That afternoon, just after sunset, three men wearing masks forced their way into the house at gunpoint. They beat and tied Blake Paulie, then took his wife.

The kidnapping was different from the others in only two ways: The kidnappers had taken their victim from a house rather than off the street; also, Brenda Paulie was the first victim who did not live in the crime-ravaged Marlow West suburb of Detroit.

Detroit detectives worked overtime, even on their days off, trying to break just one of the more than a dozen kidnapping cases. Finally, frustrated by a thousand dead-end leads as well as the investigative restraints placed on them as officers of the law, they put out a signal for help.

They knew who they wanted—if he would just come.

Most of the detectives had heard the whispered stories of an auburn-haired vigilante ex-cop who wasn't afraid to take the law into his own hands in order to bring the lawless to justice. The vigilante's methods, the detectives knew, provided him with tremendous shortcuts. They also knew the kidnappers and their gang were likely to end up dead on the street if they tried to resist the vigilante.

But considering the cruelty of their crimes, that was fine with them.

Finally, doubly sickened by the kidnapping of a pregnant

newlywed, a couple of the detectives decided it was time to get outside help. None of them, of course, even knew what the vigilante's name was, much less how to get in touch with him. So they spread the word among their connections in the underworld. As only experienced detectives could know, criminals and cops have much more in common than cops and judges ever will.

So it was in early December that Hawker got a call from his Mafia friend, Louie Brancacci. Brancacci told him the story of the kidnappings, and Hawker immediately got in touch with his friend and associate, Jacob Montgomery Hayes. Hayes, as Hawker expected, was all for his going to Detroit. Hayes's butler, Hendricks, took care of shipping out the gear he would need by a private courier truck.

Hawker drove the midnight-blue Corvette his friend Big Nick Clements had completely refurbished for him. He arrived in Detroit to find that Hendricks, as always, had done a superb job of seeing that he had a quiet, comfortable place to live as well as all the fighting hardware he could ever use.

Now, after almost two fruitless weeks of painstaking detective work, Hawker had his first break. Ironically, it was luck, blind, blind luck, that he ever noticed Brenda Paulie among the throngs of people on the Detroit sidewalks.

So now he had to find her. He couldn't allow such luck to slip away.

Hawker knew he had to find a way to get past this receptionist. He knew he had to find a reason for searching the back part of the suite. He wasn't sure he had to take off his clothes to do it.

In December, in Detroit, Hawker figured, it's cold no matter where you are.

"So," said Hawker, stalling for time, "what's the title of this movie you're making? It's not a western, is it? I love westerns."

The woman scowled at him. Her way of communicating her disapproval was to sigh. She sighed now. "A western? (Sigh.) Don't be flippant with me, all right? I don't like it. We consider the films we make to be works of art . . . art that is too complicated for your average working-class drone. We make important statements and we take our work very seriously. Understand? So, from now on, I'll ask the questions. (Sigh.) What's your name?"

"My name is Hawker. James Hawker."

"Not Jim Hawker. Not Jimmy—but *James* Hawker." The woman sighed her distaste. "I'm afraid it'll never do. You'll have to choose another."

"Another what?"

"Another name, for God's sake. Can you really be so dumb?" She looked at him and rolled her eyes. "Yes, I guess you can be. Look, I'm sure you put a lot of time into thinking up that name, and it does show a pleasant childlike imagination, but it just doesn't fit."

"Yeah, but I didn't know you were making a western. How about Roy Hawker? Randolph Hawker? Duke—"

"We are *not* making a western, and I'm getting a little tired of your inane jokes." There was a reptilian glow in the woman's eye, and Hawker guessed her hobby was cutting healthy American males into little bite-size pieces.

"Look, lady, I don't—"

7

"Don't 'look lady' me, buster!" the woman cut in. She jumped up from her desk and wagged a finger in Hawker's face. "You have three choices. You can call me Ms. Bent, or, if we hire you, you can call me Adria."

"And the third choice?" asked Hawker, trying hard to be meek.

"The third choice is to get the fuck out of here and kiss your screen test good-bye." Pushing her jaw out, the woman glared at him. The cigarette drooped from the corner of her mouth.

"Oops. Sorry. Guess I was a little out of line . . . Ms. Bent." Hawker, who hadn't known about the porno operation until he walked into the office, added, "I'd hate to blow my chances at this screen test, ma'am. I've been looking forward to this for a long, long time."

Some of the anger left the woman's face. She nodded. "That's better. I always like to let our actors know exactly where they stand from the very first day." She gave him a penetrating look. "Do you know where you stand, Mr. Hawker?"

Slumping submissively, Hawker looked at the point where his feet touched the linoleum. "I think I do, Ms. Bent. I think I know exactly where I stand."

"Good. So we need to work on a new name for you—if you look good on film, of course." She studied him closely for the first time. "What happened to your nose, for God's sake? Was it broken?"

Hawker touched his face experimentally. "Geeze, I don't think so. My face may have been shoved to the side a couple of times, but my nose is just fine."

"More jokes, huh? (Sigh.) Well, strip off those clothes, buster—then maybe we will really have something to joke about."

"Now?"

"Yes, *now!*"

Hawker wore jeans, running shoes, and a rust-colored sweater beneath a short leather jacket. The jacket was still wet from the snow that was falling outside. Hawker took his right foot in both hands and hopped around for a moment as if trying to remove his shoe. He stopped abruptly, an expression of innocence on his face. "Say, do you have a head around here?"

"A what?"

"You know, a head . . . a toilet."

The woman's face reddened. "Look, you silly little shit, if you're too shy to strip in front of me, you're sure as hell too shy to do a porno film!"

"Naw, it's not that. Whenever I get nervous, my bladder gets little cramps." He lowered his voice to a whisper. "I've got to pee."

"*Pee?*"

Hawker kicked at the floor. "I'm sorry—urinate."

The woman's face was growing redder. "It's through that door, second hallway to the left—and don't forget to put up the lid." She snapped off her last words. "And when you get back, buster, you'd better be nude. You may have time to waste, but I don't."

Hawker turned to go, then stopped. He said, "Say, Adria, while I'm gone, would you mind getting me a cup of that coffee? Cream and Sweet 'n Low if you've got it." He smiled sweetly.

The woman was just lighting another cigarette. She exhaled smoke through bared teeth.

Hawker didn't wait for her answer. He had a feeling it wasn't going to be very nice. He went through the door into the second set of offices. As he did, he touched the .45 automatic in the Jensen speed holster beneath his jacket. The weight of the weapon was reassuring.

Hawker smiled at a private joke. He was thinking: There's no way that ball-breaking bitch is going to get my clothes off me—not as long as I'm armed.

TWO

James Hawker moved quickly down the hallway.

He walked right past the door marked "Men."

He remembered what Adria Bent had said about the camera crew. She'd said they were shooting on one of the back sets. Hawker assumed that meant they were working in one of the rear offices.

He wanted to see exactly what they were working on.

For the first time since he had come to Detroit, he felt a slight trickle of confidence about the prospects of breaking at least one of the kidnapping cases.

It all figured: Pornography was a reasonable motive for kidnapping an attractive young woman. It might not be the reason why all thirteen women were taken, but it was a start—if he was right.

Hawker moved quietly through the next office. It was empty, and the few desks were covered with plastic and a layer of dust. The suite was obviously a temporary quarters for the pornographers. The offices were probably inexpensive to lease for a week or two of work. And, judging from the old building's construction, the rooms were probably all but soundproof.

Hawker paused at the next door and touched his ear to the heavy wood. From within he heard a muted *kerwack* followed by a cry of anguish.

Hawker forced himself to remain calm. He cracked the door ever so slightly and peered in. He had been confident the woman was Brenda Paulie. Now he was positive. And what he saw made him want to vomit.

They had strapped her spread-eagle to a bed, using leather thongs. The woman was completely naked, and Klieg lights and a pair of cameras hunched above her. Also on the stage were two muscular men. Both of them wore leather masks. The more muscular of the two men had a freakishly large penis, and he engaged in coitus while the woman lay helpless, her head thrown back in pain, the veins in her neck pounding, sweat beading on her forehead. The second held a leather whip. Whenever the woman seemed to resist, he slapped her sharply with the whip. She had round, heavy, milk-white breasts that now showed the iridescent red streaks of the whip. The pale nipples beaded with blood.

Hawker took a deep breath and drew the .45-caliber Colt ACP. He took note of the odds as he slid a cartridge into the chamber. There were five of them: a cameraman, a lighting grip, the director, and the two actors. The actors and the technicians would probably be trouble, Hawker decided. The director, who wore salmon-color jodhpurs and a pink shirt, would not be.

Behind the director, a woman sat on a steel folding chair. She wore a black negligee, smoked a blue cigarette, and her hair was cut into a punkish purple Mohawk. Hawker refused to even imagine how the woman with the Mohawk figured into the plot of the movie—if there was a plot.

In one swift motion, Hawker kicked the door open and stepped into the room. "Freeze! Not a word; not a move!" Then to the muscular actor who had stopped midstroke in his rape of Brenda Paulie, Hawker shouted, "You're not supposed to freeze, dumb shit! Climb down off her. *Now!* And take off those damn masks. What are you two supposed to be? Members of the Fire Island executioner's club or something?"

Hawker helped him off the woman with a sharp kick in the butt. It may not have damaged the actor's ego, but the kick certainly deflated his libido. Hawker motioned all of them against the wall as he walked toward Brenda Paulie. As he leaned down and pulled his Randall Attack/Survival knife from the scabbard on his calf, the director stepped forward.

"Who are you?" he demanded shrilly. "Are you a cop? Even if you are, you have absolutely no right to interrupt serious work in this manner. Do you have a search warrant? Do you?"

Hawker cut the leather thongs. "Do I have a search warrant?" He smiled. "Sure." He motioned with the .45 automatic in his right hand. "This is my search warrant. And if you so much as look at me wrong, you nauseating little shit, they'll be pulling chunks of your skull out of the wall until the end of this century."

"I never said you *had* to have a search warrant," the director said quickly. "And we're not moving, are we? Not even an inch. We're going to do whatever you tell us." He looked at the others. The two actors had taken off their masks, and Hawker was surprised at how young they looked. Both of them looked very frightened as they watched Hawker replace the Randall in its scabbard.

There was a sheet on the floor, and Hawker used it to cover up Brenda Paulie. For the first time, she seemed to realize she was free. Hawker could see firsthand that she had a lithe athlete's body and a pretty cheerleader's face. She opened her eyes groggily. "Are we done now? Can we go, please?"

"Yeah, Mrs. Paulie," Hawker said softly, "we can go now. I'm taking you home. Home to your husband, Blake. Home to a doctor."

The woman's head cocked slightly, as if she didn't believe what she had just heard. "Home? Home to my husband? Why are you lying to me? Please don't do that."

Hawker squeezed her wrist tenderly. "I'm not lying to you, Brenda. I'm a friend. We're going to find you some clothes and get you away from these animals."

"Home?" the woman echoed. "Oh, that would be so . . . so *nice*. That would be just wonderful. Really? You really mean it? God, I think you do." She pushed at her stringy black hair as if to neaten it for the journey—a pathetic gesture. "I've been away for so long, it seems. Such a long, long time. I know Blake has been worried about me, and I just haven't been able to call." She looked carefully at Hawker. He could see the depth of the confusion and the hysteria in her bleary eyes. She added anxiously, "You have to let me get cleaned up first. Please. You can't let Blake see me like this." She began to wring her hands as if to rid them of some unspeakable filth. "I'm just so . . . so . . . so damn *dirty* . . ." Her voice faltered and she began to cry softly, her knees pulled up to her chest in a fetal position. Brenda Paulie looked small and humiliated and tragic.

Hawker stared at the director. Hawker stared at him for a long, searing moment. He stared at him until the sweat beaded on the little man's forehead and the weak jaw quivered. Trembling, the director wore a nervous, mongrel smile. He saw something in Hawker's eyes that was cold and murderous. The director pleaded, "I didn't hire her. Honest. I help them work together. They supply the actors and I make the films—"

Hawker exhaled a long breath. The director seemed to realize how close Hawker had come to pulling the trigger. His knees wobbled and he touched a chair to balance himself. A dark stain began to spread across the crotch of the jodhpurs. The director had wet himself.

"Who brought her here?" Hawker demanded. His voice, barely audible, was a hoarse whisper. "No more bullshit, no more explanations. Just tell me."

"She . . . she's one of Queen Faith's people."

"Who?"

"Queen Faith. She's like a talent agency . . . an underground talent agency. She recruits street people. You know: drug users, poor kids, runaways. She supplies actresses."

"Women? Just women?"

The director hesitated. "Usually. But sometimes she has young boys available . . . when we need them." The director took a slow step backward. His face was now a pasty white. "Why are you looking at me like that? You certainly can't blame just me. All the filmmakers use Queen Faith. All of them. Honest. You aren't going to shoot me, are you?"

Hawker struggled against his own anger. He wanted badly to drive his fist through the face of this repulsive little creature. But emotion, he knew, was an indulgence for amateurs. He forced himself to remain stoic. "I'm not going to shoot you—as long as you keep telling me what I want to know. Understand?"

The man nodded immediately. "Anything. Anything you want."

"Is Queen Faith that bitch you've got stationed out front?"

"Adria? Certainly not—"

"Then tell me where I can find her. Tell me where I can find Queen Faith."

"Don't do it, Sol," the cameraman broke in. He looked anxiously at the director. "You know what's going to happen if you talk? You know what's going to happen to us all?"

"Do you want me to tell you what's going to happen if you don't?" Hawker snapped.

The director shuddered, his voice broke, and he began to cry. "I'll tell you." He sobbed. "I'll talk. But please . . . *please* don't hurt me. I can't tolerate pain. I really can't. Please believe me—"

"Where can I find her?" Hawker demanded. "Where can I find Queen Faith?"

The director took a deep breath. "Her operation is run out of—"

He never got a chance to finish. There was a ringing gunshot and, simultaneously, the director's face lost form, bulged grotesquely, then exploded like a shattered pumpkin.

In the back entranceway stood the pock-faced man Hawker had seen with Brenda Paulie. The black, heavy-caliber revolver he held was still smoking.

As the pistol swung toward him, Hawker dove and fired . . .

THREE

The slugs made thudding sounds above Hawker's head as his attacker got off two quick shots, then ducked back behind the fire door.

Hawker held the Colt ACP in both hands as he lay belly first on the tile floor, arms thrust outward, both eyes focused on the man in the doorway. He squeezed the trigger once, and a pockmark was punched into the soft steel.

He waited patiently for the man to return fire. But he didn't. It finally dawned on Hawker that the man was escaping.

Swearing at his own stupidity, the vigilante jumped to his feet to give chase. As he did, someone hit him from behind. It was the cameraman—a short, stocky Italian who had arms like a bear. He tackled Hawker around the waist, taking care to pin his gun hand down. Immediately the other three men tried to help wrestle Hawker to the ground.

On the bed, Brenda Paulie screamed as she watched the auburn-haired stranger who had promised her freedom now fight for his life. As she inhaled to scream again, the woman with the purple Mohawk slapped her sharply across the face then pulled her by the hair off the bed. "Shut up, you silly bitch! No one's going to help you now. *No one.*"

Brenda Paulie collapsed on the floor, sobbing uncontrollably.

But Hawker hadn't given up yet. He swung backward with his left elbow and heard the cartilage of the cameraman's nose burst. One of the actors had him around the neck while the other tried to tackle him. The lighting grip bounced around the chaotic tangle like a rooster, swinging at Hawker's face whenever he got the chance.

The vigilante had the brief mental image of a buffalo being hauled down by a pack of jackals—that's exactly the way he felt.

Hawker got in a few more good blows, but then the grip went to work on his fingers until he was forced to drop the Colt. While three of the men held him, the cameraman got the pistol and the Randall and tossed the knife to the side.

"Let him go!" the cameraman shouted as he leveled the Colt at Hawker. "Go ahead—turn him loose. Let's see how tough he is without his gun." The Italian man's nose poured blood down his chin, onto his shirt. He tried to wipe it away with the back of his wrist, but with little effect. "Why don't you try to give some orders now, smart ass? Come on! Say something! Tell me again what you're going to do if we don't obey you."

The two actors had Hawker's arms bent behind his back. Hawker gave a half shrug. "I'd rather just stand here and wait for you to bleed to death."

The cameraman slapped him with a heavy backhand. "Really like your little fucking jokes, don't you?"

"Your nose is pumping it out faster than your heart can make it, friend. Who's joking?"

"That kind of amuses you, doesn't it? Doesn't it? You broke my fucking nose, you bastard!" The cameraman lifted the Colt toward Hawker. "You broke my nose, and you got Sol killed too."

"Me? One of your people killed that little jerk. Don't blame me."

"Queen Faith's people aren't our people, asshole. The man who killed Sol wasn't with us. But you can bet he's headed back to his own people to tell them what went on here. And do you know what that means? Do you? It not only means we're left with a body to explain, but it also means we're out of the hard porn business for a while. We're going to be on Queen Faith's shit list. And, in this town, that means you might as well sell your cameras and get a job peddling insurance." The cameraman pushed his face closer to Hawker's. "It means, asshole, that you have cost us a lot of time and a lot of money."

"You don't have to explain it to him," the stockier actor said. There was a feminine breeziness in his speech, yet it was charged with emotion. "Just kill him. Go ahead. The son of a bitch deserves it. Look at the way poor Sol is lying there. Christ, it's awful the way he looks. He's got no face no more—and it's all this bastard's fault." The talk of violence caused the actor's face to flush with a heat that was unmistakably sexual.

Hawker looked over his shoulder with an expression of contempt. He said, "I bet you like car wrecks too, don't you?"

The actor put so much pressure on Hawker's arm that the vigilante was sure the ball of the shoulder joint would rip loose from its socket. "I'm tired of his smart-ass answers!" the man complained. "Shoot him now, damn it. Why wait?"

The cameraman shook his head. "I'm all for killing him. If he lives, he blows to the cops about poor little Brenda Paulie here. Even though she's one of Queen Faith's herd, we'll still get nailed for it. For kidnap and rape, even with a soft judge, you're looking at six, seven years. Killing him is the smart thing to do."

"So do it!"

The cameraman hacked and spit blood. "I just thought of a way we can have the satisfaction of killing him and *still* make money doing it. Probably more money on one project than we've ever made before."

The woman with the purple Mohawk spoke to them for the first time. She still stood guard over Brenda Paulie, but now she took a step toward the cameraman. "I think I know what you mean, Benny. I think I see what you have in mind."

"Yeah? What?"

"Film it. . . . Murder this dude and film the whole thing."

Benny grinned. "That's exactly what I mean. You remember that Rolling Stones movie back in the early seventies? The one called *Gimme Shelter?* The movie made a bundle for one reason: If you watched real close, you could see some Hell's Angel kill a guy right on film. We got the chance now to make a black-market movie that would be a hundred times better than that. A movie that would sell a hundred thousand prints the first month. We've got a chance to make the toughest

21

S-and-M film ever produced—and finish it in a way no other movie has ever ended. With a real murder."

The woman with the Mohawk smiled. "I like it, Benny. I *like* it."

Hawker listened, incredulous. He felt like a chunk of beef at a McDonald's marketing session.

Benny continued, almost as if talking to himself. "I've always wanted to direct. God knows, I've paid my dues behind that camera." He considered the carnage on the floor for a moment. "Sol always said I'd get my chance if I was just patient. Maybe I've been patient enough, huh?"

"Hell, go for it, Benny."

"Yeah, Sol won't care."

The cameraman took one more look at the bloody corpse on the floor and slapped his thigh. "By God, we're going to do it. We're going to make a movie that will make us all rich!" To the woman with the purple hair, he said, "Donna, I want you in the film with him. You'll be his costar." He chuckled. "His *last* costar—get it? We'll get him strapped to the bed, just like we had the girl. Then I want you to go down on him. You've got to get him interested, see? That's going to be the tough part. He's not going to be in the mood, but you've got to get him up. To make this movie work, it's an absolute must. Understand? And one other thing: You'll have to wear one of the masks. I don't want them to be able to recognize you. I don't want the cops nailing any of us."

The woman gave a wicked cackle. "Get him up? Baby, I could suck-start a Buick if I really put my mind to it." She strolled over to Hawker and squeezed his crotch. "Hey, surprise, surprise. It feels to me like our hero has all the necessary equipment too."

"Then what happens, Benny?" one of the actors asked. "You're gonna have Donna get him up, then just shoot him?"

The cameraman thought for a moment. He gestured toward the corpse only a few feet away. "I don't know. Shit, I wish Sol wasn't dead. He was good at this sort of thing. He could have worked it all out in his head in nothing flat."

"I think you've got to build up to some sort of climax, Benny," said the actor. "And I think the person going down on him should be the one who kills him."

"Donna, you mean?"

"Hey," the woman put in haughtily, "I didn't sign up to do no double duty. What do you want me to do? Blow him or blow him away? I ain't doing both." She brushed at her purple Mohawk, a gesture of concentration. After a moment, she added, "Tell you the truth, Benny, I'd kinda like to try shooting him. I've gone down on thousands of guys, but I ain't never killed nobody—that I know of. And it's good to try new experiences."

Hawker felt his stomach roll.

It got worse.

Behind him he heard the stockier actor say anxiously, "I'll do both, Benny. I'll go down on him and, just before it's time, I'll kill him. But I don't want to use the gun, Benny. I want to use his big silver knife you threw on the floor back there. Honest, Benny, I can do it. I'm ready for it; I've matured in my craft. All I want is a chance at some kind of signature performance. Can you picture it, Benny? Just as this dude is getting his rocks off, the camera zooms in tight. That's when I pull out the knife and open him like a melon. We get it all on film, see? The way his face looks as he dies; the way his guts pour out. And with me wearing the leather mask, the fucking S-and-M's out there will go crazy. We'll make a million bucks." The actor pressed his lips close to Hawker's ear as he added, "Plus, it will be fun."

Hawker jerked his face away. "Boy," he hissed, "if you ever touch me again, you'd better cut my head off and hide it—because that's the only thing that's going to stop me from coming after you."

The cameraman ignored him. He had found a handkerchief and was now dabbing at his ruined nose. "You're talking strictly gay market, Alex," he said, shaking his head. "I want both markets. So let's compromise. Donna, once we get him on the bed, we'll start the cameras. I want you to strip, then I want you to take his mind off everything but what you're doing. You know the bit; no one does it better than you, baby." To the stockier performer, he said, "Alex, you come on camera once Donna gets to work. Carry the knife." The cameraman smirked. "After that, do what you want. Join in any way that seems . . . interesting." He turned to Hawker. "How does that sound to you, ace?"

Hawker was angry—and scared. But he was damn determined to show neither emotion. As the men dragged him toward the bed, he heard himself say, "You can't use me in the movies. Don't you see why? Hell, my *nose*—it's too crooked, you dumb shits. Walk out to the front office and ask Adria Bent. She'll tell you."

24

In spite of his nose, the three men wrestled him to the bed and strapped him down. They tied him with pieces of the same leather thongs they had used on Brenda Paulie.

For that, at least, Hawker was thankful. The leather was about a quarter-inch thick, plenty strong enough to hold a woman. But not strong enough to hold him during the degradation they had in mind—or so he hoped.

Because of his chosen profession, Hawker had few illusions about growing to a ripe old age. He was a vigilante. A killer. And one day, no doubt, he would cross someone smarter, someone faster, someone tougher or luckier, and he would die. But now, as they tied him to the bed, he vowed not to die like this. Not to die as a degraded flesh pile of blood and bones and tissue, soiled by the leer of the sadists who now controlled him.

If he was to die, he would die fighting; he would die killing.

Strapped to the bed, he found the Klieg lights above blinding. Everyone towered over him in grim silhouette. It was a little like being on an operating table—an appropriate simile considering what they planned to do. And, ironically, they planned to do it with his own knife: the knife hand-built by Bo Randall of Randall Knives in Orlando, Florida.

The knife that had saved his life so many times would now be used to kill him . . .

FOUR

Donna, who now wore a full leather mask, stepped into view.

The mask made her look a little like a falcon. The way she strutted and mugged told Hawker the cameras were rolling.

She turned sideways to the lens, slowly unbuttoned the negligee, then stripped it off. She had small sharp breasts with very long, very dark—almost black—nipples. She massaged herself for a few moments, then unbelted her pants and slid them down over her hips. Her broad, broodmare hips intersected abruptly at the pelvic hinge, and her vagina was shaved almost smooth except for one neatly tended band of hair that ran along both sides of the vulva.

Hawker flexed his muscles against the strength of the leather thongs as the woman approached him. She ran a purple fingernail down his chest, then slid her hand up under his sweater. The snap on his jeans popped; his belt came undone; then he heard the muted growl of his zipper.

She pulled his pants down to his knees, and James Hawker felt the woman's hands on him then, felt her roll him between her small palms as if trying to warm him. Then her mouth opened wide and took him in. Hawker resisted . . . struggled to resist . . . fought desperately to resist . . . but the woman continued to lure him toward that narrow reality that consists only of the wilting suction, the flickering tongue, the heat of saliva, and the inexorable drive to deposit.

Hawker fought it. He fought it for a long time, it seemed. Sweat rolled down his forehead and thighs, and the musky odor of naked, sweating, wanting woman was overpoweringly in his face. Every time he slid away from her, the searching, seeking, vacuum mouth found him again and swallowed him like a creature alive. He kept telling himself that to submit was to give in to the most perverted, degrading experience of his life.

But the body sometimes has a mind of its own. And, finally, his body began to turn traitor. It began to react to the wants of the mouth that sought him. It began to react to the heat and smell and damnable suction.

It was at that moment, out of the corner of his eye, Hawker saw the husky male actor approaching. Alex was obviously aroused—but not by the scent of sex. It was the scent of death that drew him now, and in his eyes was the perverse joy of having an opportunity to slaughter.

In his right hand was the bright star-glimmer of the stainless steel attack/survival knife.

Alex drew it high overhead. Wearing the leather mask, he looked like an Aztec priest about to sacrifice a virgin.

Then he drove the knife down; downward with a *whoof* of effort, driving it toward the heart of the man beneath him.

Hawker unleashed all his strength, all his weight, against the leather bindings. Those holding his ankles snapped, as did the thong holding his right wrist. But the strap on his left hand refused to give.

Even so, it was enough. He kicked upward with his knees, hitting Donna in the side of the head. With the tenacity of an Electrolux, she clung for a moment before somersaulting away. Hawker suppressed a roar of agony as he rolled off the bed just as the seven-and-a-half–inch stainless steel blade drove through the mattress.

"Keep it rolling!" Benny yelled to the lighting grip, who now stood at the second camera. Delighted by what was happening, Benny paced away from his station—and almost tripped over the body of Sol, the director. "Realism," he yelled. "Realism! It's exactly what we want now, Alex! It's the statement we want to make. Keep the action going!"

All the realism James Hawker wanted was to get the hell away from these lunatics. He pulled violently on the thong, dragging the whole bed as Alex slashed at him with the knife. Donna, with her purple Mohawk bristling and the right side of her face swollen, was on her feet again. She screamed, "Kill that dirty puke, Alex! Cut his guts out!"

As Alex lunged at him, Hawker lurched backward—and the thong snapped. The naked actor tumbled over him, and the vigilante got to his knees and cracked him flush in the face with a sizzling right fist. The knife flew into the air as Alex fought groggily to get to his feet. Hawker snatched up the knife and, holding his pants with his left hand, drew it back with every intention of putting Alex's mask on the floor without taking it off his head.

But then there were two deafening explosions, and Hawker turned to see that Donna had somehow found his .45 automatic. Naked, she held it awkwardly in both hands. "I'll kill you myself, you son of a bitch! Nobody kicks me and gets away with it!"

Once again she fired, and one of the Klieg lights shattered high above his head.

Benny was still at his camera, as was the lighting grip. Both of them panned to follow Hawker as he dove over the bed and rolled toward Donna. At that range he expected the next shot to hit him, no matter how bad a marksman she was.

But the next shot never came. Brenda Paulie had gotten to her feet, and body-blocked the woman from behind. Even so, Donna had not dropped the Colt. Hawker charged her, but the second actor—the one who had used the whip earlier—intercepted him. He tried to hit Hawker with a massive roundhouse, but Hawker ducked under it and knocked him off his feet with a straight right to the throat. The actor went down, gagging.

Realizing for the first time that Hawker really might escape, Benny and the lighting grip left their cameras as if on cue. Donna was still trying to fix the sights of the .45 on him, so, when Brenda Paulie threw open the door and yelled, "Run!" that's exactly what Hawker did.

He pushed the girl through before him, slammed the door, and pulled a desk in front of it.

From inside, a muffled shot splintered the heavy wood.

Hawker took Brenda Paulie by the elbow and together they ran through the bank of empty offices, down the hall, and through the door into the front offices.

Adria Bent jumped up from her desk in surprise. "Where in the hell did you go? You have absolutely no right to roam around this place unattended! You can just forget your film test, *friend.*"

Quickly Hawker did three things in succession: He locked the door behind him; he painfully snapped his pants; he returned the Randall knife to its scabbard. There was an evil expression on his face, but Adria Bent refused to be intimidated.

"I'm tempted to call some of my employees out here and have them kick the shit out of you. That's the only thing people like you understand—"

"Shut up," Hawker snapped. He considered the wraparound skirt she wore. "And take off that dress—*now.*"

"Are you mad?"

"I'm beyond mad, lady. I'm genuinely pissed off. So you take off that skirt without another word and give it to that nice girl holding the sheet around her."

Adria Bent's eyes grew wide. "Hey, she's one of our people. You can't take her—"

In one motion, Hawker grabbed the skirt and stripped it off her. The force spun the woman around like a top until she fell heavily against the desk.

Hawker tossed the skirt to Brenda. "Can you get into that?"

"Sure. I can tie it in front."

"And take my jacket too."

She let the sheet fall, and Hawker saw once again how badly the whip had scarred her breasts.

Wearing only a blouse and panties, Adria Bent was turning

a deep shade of red—not from embarrassment, from anger. "You *touched* me, you bastard! No man touches me, do you understand . . ."

Hawker ignored her screaming and opened the front door. "We'd better go," he said to Brenda Paulie. "Running wouldn't hurt—if you can run."

"I'm . . . I'm so tired."

"I know. Just hang on for a little while longer. Once we get outside, I'll call your husband and we'll get you to a doctor."

"And for you too. You're sort of limping. I can tell you're hurt. Did she . . . did she shoot you?"

"Almost as bad. Did you see what she was doing when I kicked her?"

"No."

"Well, I'm not walking funny because she shot me."

"Oh? Oh!"

From behind them came a feverish pounding on the door. Hawker pushed the girl out into the hall toward the elevator. He stepped through, then peeked back into the office.

To a fuming Adria Bent he said, "By the way, doll, you can forget about that coffee. I'm just not in the mood anymore."

FIVE

"Hello?"

"Well, well, if it isn't James Hawker, the famous mystery man."

"Famous mystery man? Can there be such a thing?"

"Mix a vigilante with a porno star and, *voilà*, you have a famous mystery man."

"Ah!"

"Pretty clever, huh?"

"They don't call you Detective Sergeant Paul McCarthy for nothing."

"What a coincidence that you should bring up my official position. I'm calling on official business."

"Gee, what an honor. Let me guess: You've finished your interview with Brenda Paulie, and now you want me to fill in all the hazy details, all the ambiguous wording so you can take full credit for busting a case that has been puzzling the experts for years."

"Years?"

"Well, months."

"Nineteen months, to be exact. And it's still puzzling the experts—but we are glad to get Brenda Paulie back. The press is demanding to know why the details of her escape are so sketchy. For some reason, the idea of an unnamed private citizen pulling off a major rescue operation, then quietly disappearing into the crowd, has captured the public's imagination. Did you see the *Free Press* this morning? It called you the 'phantom hero.'"

"Yeah? 'Phantom hero,' huh? The guy who said that journalism is the lowest form of prose may have been right. The press isn't actively searching for this phantom, is it?"

"You got me. But just for the record, there's no way in the world I could take credit for the rescue—not that I wouldn't love to." He chuckled. "Believe me, I've considered all the angles. The Detroit Police Department doesn't exactly come out smelling like a rose on this one. We could use a morale boost in this case."

As they talked, Hawker sat in his rented bungalow not far from Jefferson Beach on the shore of Lake St. Clair. The bungalow had the sparse, vacation furniture of a summer house. In the stone fireplace, black logs hissed beneath translucent flames. Through the window, Hawker could see the gray beach beneath the gray sky and the winter expanse of the lake. He said into the phone, "There's no way the department can come out looking good on this case, Paul. Hell, don't blame yourself. To break it, you would have to keep shaking the tree until someone inside turned informer. Then once you got the information you needed, you would have to go through the courts to get the search warrants and the wire taps necessary to build a case. Once there was sufficient evidence, then—and only then—could you do a proper bust and free the kidnap victims. That would take months. And the citizenry doesn't like sitting around on its thumbs while high-school girls and young mothers are being raped, sodomized, and forced to have group sex in porno films. Either way, you're the bad guys."

Paul McCarthy chuckled. "So what else is new?"

"Valid point."

"Yeah. Yeah, it is a valid point. I guess that's why we had to do it, Hawk. That's why a couple of other nameless detectives and I finally took a stand. When we finally decided we needed your help, it was like telling the system to go screw itself"—he laughed again—"privately, of course."

"Oh, yeah?"

"Yeah. Stupid of us, probably, but we did it anyway. See, we'd heard all these neat rumors about some auburn-haired hot shot terrorizing bad asses all around the country. We heard he hit the street gangs in L.A. and blew apart some kind of commie revolutionaries down in Florida. Like most the cops in this country, the grapevine told us about his sticking it to the Libyans in Vegas and some right-winger down in Texas. So we made up our minds to get in touch with this superman and see if we couldn't get him in here, convince him to skip all the legalities, and just kick the ass of these sickos before they brutalized someone again."

Hawker played along. "Yeah. And you were very convincing."

"Until I finally saw you. Then I wasn't so sure I wanted to be convincing. Turns out superman looks more like an auburn-haired James Garner—but uglier. A lot uglier."

"Hah!"

"It's true. And instead of wading in with a club, he sits back for two weeks working at his computer and going over files and memorizing photographs. Turns out our superman—this notorious rogue cop who is fast becoming a national legend—is just like any other cop, only he works harder."

"And I'm lucky," Hawker put in.

"Yeah, you're lucky. And I'd rather be lucky than good. Say, Hawk, how did you track down Brenda Paulie, anyway?"

"I didn't. I was downtown and crossed the street to buy a steak-on-the-stick from a vendor, and there she was."

"Just like that? You picked her out of the crowd?"

"No, first I picked out the jerk who was pimping her. Had that look about him. You know: nervous eyes, fidgety hands, chip on his shoulder. Then I took a close look at her. The trick to memorizing people from their photos is to look at the photo and see them as they'd look completely bald. Even then, I wasn't sure. So I followed them. You know the rest. I called you right after I called an ambulance for Brenda. How's she doing?"

"After only twenty-four hours of freedom, she's doing damn well—physically, anyway. The doctors are still going over her, but they say she's going to make it. They said you didn't get her out of there any too soon. She lost the baby, of course, and there is a real danger of peritonitis. Emotionally she seems to be holding up, but the doctors have already gotten her into therapy. That poor girl has taken more abuse and been through more shit in the last three months than most of us get in a lifetime. She's going to need help. Lots of it. Her husband seems to be a nice guy. He's hanging right in there."

Hawker said, "Did she tell you any more about Queen Faith? Anything at all?"

"That's what I'm calling you about. I may have a chance to nail that bitch. Any possibility of your meeting us for dinner this evening?"

"Us?"

"Yeah. Detective Sergeant Riddock and me."

"I haven't met Detective Riddock, have I?"

"No, but you will tonight. Do you like ritzy food or cheap?"

"I like all food. Let's make it ritzy—on me."

"A freebee? You know we're not allowed to accept any gifts."

"Is that a 'no'?"

"No, it's a 'yes.'" Paul McCarthy laughed. "Hey, I guess it's true what they say. Once a cop goes bad, it just keeps getting easier and easier."

SIX

Wearing sweatpants and a stocking cap, Hawker went for a long run. He stuck to the beach as far as he could, then had to cut up and get on the back streets because of the rugged shoreline.

It was late afternoon, a time of eerie, desert light. A raw northeast wind whirled the snow into dust devils and blew the tops off the endless rows of waves. Seagulls on the drab sky soared out of control.

As Hawker ran, he tried to think of a way to get inside the Queen Faith organization. He had been lucky once. But he couldn't count on luck to see him through again.

He needed facts. Cold, hard data. And the sooner he got it, the better.

Back in his bungalow, Hawker put more wood on the fire then stripped off his running clothes. The floor was tile, cold beneath his feet. He wrapped a towel around himself, opened a Tuborg dark, and carried it to the shower.

Half an hour later, he was driving in fast traffic on Woodward Avenue, headed out of the city. Detroit was getting ready for Christmas. Plastic Santas waved from used car lots, and the anticrime vapor lights were strung with red ribbon and topped with candy canes to proclaim the season of love and goodwill. On every busy street corner, women of strong faith, virginal in their dark cloaks, stood by Salvation Army kettles and clanked bells for the souls of the lost and homeless—winos, mostly.

The snow had turned to cold drizzle. Gray clouds permeated all space between sky and earth, so smokestacks and skyscrapers were only partially visible, like the tops of mountains. Traffic was an unbroken blur of headlights; the road glistened; driving was treacherous. Hawker kept his hands at the ten-and-two position on the steering wheel of his midnight-blue Corvette fastback. He spun the radio dial past a dozen different screaming rock-and-soul stations until he finally came to an oldies program. WOWO, Fort Wayne, Indiana. Farm country.

His spirit had begun to match the drabness of the evening. But then the WOWO disc jockey played a knockout three-some: "Don't Worry Baby" by The Beach Boys; "Popsicles, Icicles" by The Mermaids; "Once in My Life" by The Righteous Brothers.

By the middle of the first song. Hawker was tapping his foot. By the end of the third song, he was singing out loud, pounding out the bass part on the steering wheel.

He turned the oldies program up full blast, and by the time he got to the restaurant he was feeling good again, grinning even.

The name of the restaurant was The Three Sisters. To

Hawker's surprise, it was in a converted barn with a converted barnyard for a parking lot. It was a Wednesday night but the lot was nearly filled. Hawker took it as a good sign.

The interior of the restaurant was right out of a *Saturday Evening Post* pictorial. Rough-hewn oak tables were covered with clean white tablecloths and there were bales of hay in the loft.

Paul McCarthy sat alone at a corner table. Hawker had met him only once before, but he realized again that McCarthy looked less like a cop than he did the junior partner of some respected law firm. McCarthy wore a navy blazer and gray worsted slacks. The grin was boyish and the brown hair—worn stylishly long—seemed to represent a personal balance between the excesses of the late sixties and the responsibilities of the eighties. He stood when he saw Hawker and waved him over.

"The legend walks," McCarthy chided, "but is the legend hungry?"

"Don't let your hand stray near my mouth or you may lose it. Is the food any good here? Or did we just come for the cosmopolitan atmosphere?"

"Hey, don't knock The Three Sisters yet. Let me tell you about the place. Three Amishmen started it. Built the barn themselves, put in the kitchen, actually milled the wood to make the tables. Almost all the food they serve here comes off the farms from an Amish community outside Pontiac. They make their own breads, pies, everything." McCarthy closed his eyes momentarily in an attitude of reverence. "And James, James, the beef is . . . is heavenly. It's the best. Period.

It is unbelievable. They feed the steers especially for the table. Hand-feed them nothing but corn and—here's their secret—homemade beer."

"Beer?"

"Great, huh? A quart a day. All that barley and malt really fattens 'em up. Keeps them happy too. The Amish can't drink it, so they feed it to their private herd. The results, James, are beyond description. It didn't take long for the word to get around, so the place started filling up. It got so popular that the Amish families finally decided to just tend to producing the food and overseeing the kitchen, and turned the rest of the responsibilities over to a manager. The quality of the food didn't go down, but now they can serve alcohol. Speaking of which . . ."

Hawker signaled the waitress and ordered a bull-shot because of the cold and a Strohs because beer was his favorite drink. She placed menus in front of them, smiled, then walked off wag-hipped toward the kitchen.

Hawker stirred the alcohol into the beef bullion then took a sip of the bullshot. "So where is Detective Riddock? I thought he was having dinner with us."

McCarthy's expression was unusual. Hawker thought it a mixture of confusion and amusement. He said, "Riddock's always late. It's a character flaw. But it's good in a way, because I want to talk to you first."

"Sure."

McCarthy studied the scotch in its heavy crystal tumbler. "First, I need to fill you in on what happened when we showed up at the porno offices on East Jefferson."

"Let me guess: The body was gone." Hawker smiled.

"Wrong. The body was still there. The dead man's name arrived from the coroner via fingerprinting: Solomon Goldblatz, alias Solly Golden, alias Steven Grosvenor—"

"Steven Grosvenor?"

"There's a little bit of the wistful WASP in all of us."

"Ah."

"Goldblatz was a small-time crook but a really big-time slime. I'm talking about a real major-league puke. Officially, he was mostly a con man. There were several characters he used. One was the brilliant researcher who needed backers before he could go ahead with the experiments that would make his investors rich. What he was supposedly trying to discover varied, but usually it was a cure for arthritis or cancer. He and his people kept an eye on the obituary columns, and when someone with money died, Goldblatz was at the widow's door before the body was cold in the ground."

"And the donations were usually much bigger when the deceased died of the Big C."

"Right."

"Charming guy."

"Yeah. Another one of his characters was a paternal IRS man. He would accuse people of tax fraud—everyone thinks they're guilty of tax fraud—and then he would pretend to be sympathetic about their circumstances. For a cash contribution to his favorite charity—himself—Goldblatz would agree to overlook their offense. It was a good racket, because he made the people he conned believe that, by bribing him, they had become accessories to a crime. And they sure as hell weren't going to turn themselves in."

"Pretty smart."

"Oh, yeah, he was shrewd. But, like I said, he was real slime."

"There are a lot of con men around, Paul."

"Not like Goldblatz. He was not only a con man, he was a kink. One of the real sickos."

"You're telling me? I saw the bastard in action."

"But you didn't see him in high gear. Goldblatz had been directing porno movies for years. He liked rough stuff. It helped him get his rocks off. But he liked something a lot more than violence."

"Yeah?"

"Yeah. Goldblatz was a child molester, Hawk. Calling him a rapist would be more accurate. He was never sent up for it, but he was arrested three times. Twice the parents of the children refused to allow their kids to testify. The third time, the kid went into a catatonic retreat, like a zombie, and there were no other witnesses. Goldblatz's defense attorney tore the case to shreds in the chambers. Goldblatz never even spent a day in court, let alone jail."

"I'm suddenly real sorry I wasn't the one who blew him away. I had the chance. I decided to give him a break. And I'm real sorry I didn't take care of his friends too. I've met a lot of twisted folks in my time, but these people were beyond belief. We're talking certifiable. Did you get a make on any of them?"

"No. Wish we had. They had cleared out by the time we got our people there. They took everything that might have given us some clue to their identity. All they left was a couple of empty beds, some movie lights, and Goldblatz's corpse. We've had the place dusted for prints. But so far Goldblatz is the only one we have on record. I'm surprised they had time to get the cameras out. We got there quick."

"They seemed to be pretty well organized. But then, most big-profit crime is well organized. Did your people find out anything about this woman called Queen Faith?"

McCarthy swirled his glass of scotch; the amber liquid became a violent whirlpool. "First of all, I'd heard her name before you mentioned it to me. As you know, Detective White and I and some others have been working on this case for the last six months in our spare time. All we knew was that women from the suburb of Marlow West were disappearing—we had no idea where they were being taken or why. For all we knew, a serial murderer was at work. So, to give ourselves an efficient modus operandi, we came up with a variety of motives for why someone would want to undertake a fairly large-scale kidnapping operation. By narrowing down those motives, we could make our investigation more efficient . . ." McCarthy chuckled and sipped his drink. ". . . and that's real important when you're doing that investigating on your days off."

"It sounds to me like Detroit has its share of very smart and very dedicated cops, Detective McCarthy."

"There's no amount of flattery that's going to make me pick up the check tonight."

"I had to try."

Both men laughed. "Okay," McCarthy continued, "where was I? Oh, yeah: how I heard about this creature known as Queen Faith. One of the motives we came up with was kidnapping for the purposes of forced participation in pornography. Of course, until you stumbled on Brenda Paulie, Hawk, we had no idea that that is what they were doing. Anyway, Detective White and I checked out the porno angle. We made the rounds of the sleazy joints and didn't come up with much. I heard the name Queen Faith mentioned a couple of times, but I got the impression she ran some kind of second-class whorehouse. A small-timer. But then I heard about her again—when I was checking the late Sol Goldblatz's record."

"Yeah?"

McCarthy looked troubled. "Yeah. One of the kids Goldblatz assaulted gave the police a fair amount of detailed information before the parents decided the kid should have nothing to do with prosecuting the bastard. In the text of the statement, the kid mentioned a woman . . . a woman called 'Queenie.' According to the kid, Queenie was worse than just sick. She was a real freak. She got her hands on the kid before Goldblatz did. And what Queenie did really hits the nausea button." He looked at Hawker carefully. "Maybe I should wait until after dinner to tell you."

Hawker shook his head. "No. Let's hear it now."

As McCarthy described the sexual proclivities of Queen Faith, Hawker stared coldly into his beer. When McCarthy was done, Hawker drained the bottle and set it down harder than he had planned. "And you think Queenie and Queen Faith are the same woman?"

"That would be my guess," McCarthy said. "The chances of there being two women named Queen in the porno business, both of whom know Goldblatz, are pretty damn slim."

"Yeah," said Hawker thoughtfully. After a long silence,

he finally asked, "Paul, that kid you told me about. The one Queen Faith got her hands on. Was the kid a—"

"The kid was a seven-year-old girl, Hawk. And what was done to that baby would be enough to put a female adult into the loonie bin for a year. And to have it done to her by a woman . . ." He let his voice trail off.

All traces of emotion had left James Hawker's face. McCarthy observed with a chill the degree of coldness in the searing blue eyes, and he realized with some surprise that they were the eyes of a killer, a perfect, machinelike killer.

Upon reflection, McCarthy wondered why he had been surprised.

James Hawker said softly, "When I find Queen Faith, I will mention that little girl to her. It will be the last thing the bitch hears before she dies . . ."

SEVEN

Peering at their menus, the two men were about to order when Hawker noticed a woman talking to the hostess. She was pointing at them.

"Expecting a date to join you?" Hawker asked.

McCarthy chuckled. "Nope. Not a date."

The woman nodded and walked toward their table. Hawker couldn't help watching her. She was medium height, about five six, maybe a little taller. She had long golden-blond hair, a stern Germanic face that softened somewhat around the eyes and lips—the effect of which was to make her look like a very pretty teenager concerned with the world situation. Hawker guessed her to be about twenty-seven. She wore a pale tweed skirt that came to her knees, a sweater over a white blouse, and a handsome Irish woven suit jacket. Her purse was tucked under her arm like a briefcase, and she walked purposefully, as if trying to subdue the natural roll and sway of her hips. Her body was an intriguing combination of long legs, grace-ful arms, slim hips, wide shoulders, and full breasts. Hawker couldn't remember when he had seen a woman for whom he felt a stronger and more immediate physical wanting.

"You're sure you're not expecting anyone but Detective Riddock?"

McCarthy was watching the blond now. "Absolutely sure."

Hawker returned to his menu. "Too bad. But you'd hardly expect a cop to attract a woman like that. She's strictly Learjets and Mediterranean vacations."

McCarthy smiled. "Yeah. And she's probably a bitch anyway."

Hawker chuckled. It was the old bull-session version of sour grapes. Whenever a group of guys saw a beautiful woman who was obviously out of their reach, they comforted themselves by saying she was no doubt a bitch—something no one, of course, really believed. It was, in fact, a spoof of their own feelings of inadequacy; a joke on themselves that no one tired of laughing at because they were all in the same boat and, worse, it was true. McCarthy was obviously a veteran of the jock bull sessions, and Hawker felt more comfortable with him because of it.

Still grinning into his menu, Hawker played his part. "Yep, a bitch. No doubt about it: The blonde is probably a first-class bitch."

A shadow darkened his menu: The waitress had arrived to take their orders. Hawker looked up. Just as quickly, he looked back down.

It wasn't the waitress. It was the blonde. She stood behind him, a strained expression on her face. Her lips were tight and her eyes glittered. She had obviously overheard him.

Hawker cleared his throat. He could hear Paul McCarthy

laughing heavily behind his menu. Hawker shook his head and said to no one in particular, "What in the world could this be in my mouth? . . . Why . . . it's my very own shoe. Wait, I'll get it out—"

"Don't trouble yourself," the woman said.

McCarthy's face was scarlet, and he was waging a tremendous inner battle against the hysteria of laughter. Laughter, unfortunately, was winning. His whole body shook. "James Hawker," he managed to say, "allow me to introduce Detective Sergeant Claramae Riddock."

Hawker was stunned. *"What?"*

McCarthy found the question hysterical. He buried his head in his arms and sobbed.

"What?" Hawker repeated.

"I'm Detective Sergeant Claramae Riddock," the woman said tersely. "I'm with the legal department of the Detroit Police Department." She cast a look of disapproval at McCarthy. "I thought I was invited to discuss police matters. Instead I arrive just in time to hear a stranger discussing me in the basest and most offensive terms."

Hawker was still backpedaling. "Clara*mae?*" he asked, not sure anyone could possibly be named such a thing.

"That's right," the woman said in the same cold tone, "but I think you'd better call me Detective Riddock."

"Claramae!" McCarthy roared, settling into new spasms. "Oh, God." He gasped. "Why isn't someone writing this stuff down?"

People at other tables were beginning to stare.

Hawker stood. "Claramae—Detective Riddock, I'm very sorry. I mean that. I won't try to explain what I said—"

"Please don't."

"Look, my name is James Hawker. I'm a friend of Paul's. Why don't you sit down and we can talk?"

"I really don't see much sense in that, Mr. Hawker." The look of being unsettled was quickly leaving her face, replaced by an attitude of disdain. "Frankly, I find such chauvinistic attitudes beyond my understanding and far beyond my bounds of sympathy. That you find it funny, Paul, I find particularly offensive."

Through streaming eyes, McCarthy looked up long enough to say, "Don't blame me—he's the one . . . he's the one who called you a *bitch*." The young detective was immediately swamped again by his own laughter. He was now holding his sides painfully.

"Thanks a lot, Paul," Hawker said dryly. He drew out a chair for the woman, adding, "Look, I don't know why Paul wanted you here, but I'm sure it was important. You caught us in the middle of a private joke—a joke that was in bad taste, I agree. But if your ego is so delicate that you can't even be joked about, then maybe you have no business being a cop. Believe me, if you're that sensitive, the case Paul has been talking about is way out of your league."

"Don't try to manipulate me," the woman snapped. "Spare me the inane psychological tactics. I'll stay for dinner because I told Paul I would. Whatever else Detective McCarthy may be, he's a good cop. If he wants to talk to me, then I will happily listen. If, for some reason, he wants me to discuss something with you, I'll discuss it." Her voice grew sharper. "But it will not be because of any cleverness on your part, and it will not be because you somehow 'handled' me." She put her hands on her hips. "Do you understand me?"

The look of embarrassment had slowly drained from Hawker's face. His blue eyes were now cold orbs. He said softly, "Lady, I wouldn't give a micro-ounce of spittle for the privilege of understanding you. If you want to stay—stay. But if you plan to lecture me, then you'd better leave and leave quickly. I may be one of the few men you've ever met who really does believe in equality—and if you talk to me again the way you just did, I'll treat you the way I'd treat a man. Do you understand?"

Hawker and the woman were still glowering at each other when McCarthy came up for another breath of air. Rubbing his eyes, he said gaily, "Something told me you two would get along. I don't know why. Maybe it's because you remind me of each other." The laughter began to heave in him once again. "God, I ought to be a matchmaker."

"Yeah," said the woman. In unison, she and Hawker added, "At Madison Square Garden."

EIGHT

At first, there was little doubt in Hawker's mind he could win the woman over to his side.

He was mistaken.

Detective Claramae Riddock sat at the table next to Hawker, yet she insisted on staying stern, aloof, and business-like, a million miles away.

Hawker found it all the more troubling because the physical attraction he felt for her had increased rather than lessened. Sitting so close to her, Hawker could see that her skin had a healthy, coppery quality, as if her flesh had been sunbrowned, then sprinkled with metallic flakes. Her breasts pushed heavily against the material of her blouse and sweater, and her gray eyes, framed by the long golden hair, gave the woman a haunting, ethereal beauty. The physical impact she produced was almost primal. It made him want to possess her, to dominate her, to do anything he had to do to bed her.

That, he realized wryly, was not very likely considering the circumstances.

He tried small talk while they ate, but it amounted to nothing. McCarthy had regained control of himself and seemed in an unusually good mood. He seemed to be enjoying the effect Claramae Riddock was having on Hawker.

Hawker couldn't deny that it was real. He also couldn't deny that McCarthy had been absolutely correct in his judgment of The Three Sisters restaurant. He, McCarthy, and Riddock all ordered steaks. Hawker got the sixteen-ounce porterhouse. It was served on a wooden platter. On the outside, the steak was dry and scorched almost black—not particularly appetizing. But when Hawker cut into it, it was like no piece of beef he had ever eaten. The interior was beautifully rare, tender and moist beyond belief.

They ate in silence for a while. Hawker could tell there was something on McCarthy's mind. The vigilante had said nothing about the Queen Faith case, leaving it all up to the Detroit detective.

For all Claramae Riddock knew, Hawker was a reporter for a crime magazine.

As it turned out, that's exactly what McCarthy should have told her. But he didn't.

Finally, when they had all finished their steaks and were lingering over coffee and dessert, McCarthy said, "Hawk, Detective Riddock is one of the few cops around you'll find who is also a lawyer."

Trying to be as pleasant as he could, Hawker nodded as if impressed.

McCarthy continued, "Yesterday she expressed some interest in the Brenda Paulie case—"

"More accurately," the woman interrupted, "I had some serious questions about what actually happened at that porno studio. For instance, I find Brenda Paulie's story very difficult to accept. She apparently claims that some mysterious stranger interrupted the filming, fought with her captors, then spirited her away. After calling for medical help, this phantom disappeared. Furthermore, Ms. Paulie insists she cannot describe her rescuer, yet she insists that her rescuer did not shoot the dead man, Mr. Solomon Goldblatz." She looked closely at Hawker, then at McCarthy. "But frankly, Paul, I'm very uncomfortable continuing with this line of discussion unless I find out exactly how your friend figures into this investigation."

To Hawker she said, "Are you a policeman?"

"No. No, I'm not."

"Are you a journalist somehow interested in how these cases are handled?"

Hawker looked meaningfully at McCarthy. He couldn't believe the Detroit cop had brought an outsider onto the case. It put Hawker into one hell of an uncomfortable spot. McCarthy seemed to be enjoying Hawker's discomfort, so Hawker decided to turn the tables.

He decided to tell her the truth. He decided to put it to her so frankly that she would refuse to believe it.

He said, "Actually, Ms. Riddock, what I am may surprise you." (McCarthy waggled his eyebrows at that.) "I'm a vigilante." (McCarthy's smile vanished.) "I hunt down criminals and kill them." (McCarthy's expression became one of incredulity—then horror.) "My reason for being a vigilante is simple: Local law enforcement agencies are handcuffed by the restraints placed upon them by courts that serve only to protect the criminal. They're the same courts that leave the victim helpless. I go in and, in effect, wage covert war against criminal elements." Hawker glanced at McCarthy to see if he was squirming. He was. It was exactly what he wanted. McCarthy had had his little joke, now Hawker was having his. He continued, "It's violent work. Exceedingly violent. I don't waste time reading rights or worrying about what the press or the courts are going to say about me. On the streets, it's kill or be killed." Hawker smiled at the way McCarthy's eyes widened when he added, "So far I've been lucky. I've been wounded a few times, but nothing that kept me in the hospital for more than a month or so." He nodded at the woman. "That's what I do, Detective Riddock, and I hope that explains why Paul invited me to dinner tonight."

For the moment, the woman seemed too shocked to say a word. But McCarthy managed. "Ha-ha." He chortled. "Ha-ha-ha." Now that he wanted to laugh, he couldn't. "What a kidder this guy is! Boy, James, that was a good one—a vigilante. God, what an imagination." He nudged the woman. "Didn't I tell you he was a million laughs?"

"No," the woman said, "you told me no such thing. In fact, you didn't really tell me anything about your friend at all." She looked closely at Hawker, her eyes like lasers. "And obviously Paul didn't tell you much about me either, did he? You see, Mr. Hawker, I'm detective sergeant in the legal division of the D.P.D.—I'm an attorney, as Paul said. When I heard about the strange circumstances surrounding the escape of Ms. Brenda

Paulie, I immediately decided an investigation was in order."
She looked sharply at McCarthy. "A *separate* investigation.
You see, I didn't like anything about that rescue operation.
The whole thing stinks. A private citizen breaks into a porno
ring without due process, without proper warrants, without
even apprising the office inhabitants of their rights? Come on,
give some of us credit. We're not *dumb*, for God's sake. I knew
what happened from the first moment I heard the story."

"Yeah?" said Hawker, amused.

"Yes," said Claramae Riddock. "I knew rogue cops were
involved."

"Or a vigilante?"

McCarthy slapped his hand on the table a little too hard.
"Come on, Claramae, you don't really believe he's a vigilante?"

"I believe every word he just said." She looked at Hawker.
"You didn't expect me to believe you, did you? You thought
the truth would be too bizarre for me to accept."

Hawker shrugged. "So now that you know, what are you
going to do?"

"This morning I told Detective McCarthy I was going to
ask for an internal investigation and press charges if I found
any evidence of vigilante behavior on the part of members of
our force. And that's still what I plan to do—only now it will
be easier. Much easier."

"Come on, *Detective*," McCarthy snapped. "Get off your
white horse. When you told me you planned an investigation,
I thought James might be able to talk a little sense into you—
that's why I invited you here. I thought you might change your
mind when you saw what kind of guy he is."

"Change my mind? From what I've seen, Paul, your friend is rude, egotistical, ruthless, and a complete boor. Why should that change my mind?"

McCarthy's face was getting red. "He saved Brenda Paulie's life, for one thing," he said. "That doesn't mean anything to you? He's provided us with our first lead on one hell of a tough case. And he's willing to keep working with us. Now why would you want to spoil that?"

"He also violated the human rights of everyone involved with that porno ring," Claramae Riddock shot back. "He killed Solomon Goldblatz in cold blood—a man who had never been found guilty of a crime—"

"Goldblatz was a kink, for Christ's sake! He raped children."

"He was never found guilty in a court of law." She glared at McCarthy. "In this country, you're still innocent until proven guilty."

"The kids' parents wouldn't let them testify."

"Then that's the parents' problem, not the problem of the Detroit Police Department. In the eyes of the law, Mr. Goldblatz was innocent. And for Mr. Hawker to kill him is murder, plain and simple."

"I didn't kill him," Hawker interrupted coolly. "But I wish I had." He gave the woman a look of appraisal. "Tell me, Detective Riddock, have you done much work in the field?"

"I'm not on trial here, Mr. Hawker."

"Sidestepping the question?"

"Not at all. My job is strictly internal affairs. I'm not ashamed of it."

"You've never been shot at, or had to shoot someone?"

"Of course not."

"You've never worked the streets—the streets where any one of a hundred people would love to slit your throat just for the fun of it? You've never been in the pits with the crooks and killers and the rapists? I'd love to take you out some evening and introduce you to some of these fine, decent law-abiding folks you're so hellbent on protecting."

"Now who's lecturing, Hawker? I've met plenty of criminals. I work with them every day. That's why I know that they're usually just people a little more unfortunate than you and I, just people who have had some bad breaks. They're not animals and they're not freaks. They've made mistakes, but they still have rights—rights that must be protected."

"And what about the victims?"

"Once the law has been broken, there's not much a cop can do for the victim. It's unfortunate, but that's the way it is."

Hawker finished his beer and prepared to leave. He looked at McCarthy. "Paul, it has been a *lovely* evening. But I think I'd better go now before I lose my temper and tell Detective Riddock what a naive little airhead she really is."

Hastily the woman put her purse on the table and unzipped it. Hawker couldn't quite believe it when she pulled out a nickel-plated .38 police special. She pointed it at Hawker. "You're not going anywhere, mister. I'm placing you under arrest for the murder of Solomon Goldblatz."

Hawker smiled his disbelief. "Because of what we said here tonight? Come on, lady, it's your word against the two of us."

Just as calmly, she reached into her purse and produced a tiny tape recorder. The reels were turning. Detective Sergeant Claramae Riddock smiled. "Say what you want about me, Mr. Hawker, but I am no airhead." She switched off the recorder. "Properly introduced, I think I have enough here to put you and McCarthy behind bars for a long, long while . . ."

NINE

Hawker found himself paying the bill for a woman who fully intended to send him to prison. It made him feel even more ridiculous.

She put the gun away when McCarthy solemnly promised the two of them would accompany her peacefully to the station house. One by one they filed through the restaurant door. McCarthy looked at the vigilante and rolled his eyes as if to apologize. Hawker smiled. "If it makes you feel any better, Paul, that was the best steak I've ever had in my life."

He chuckled grimly. "If Annie Oakley there gets you sentenced to the electric chair, we'll know just what to bring you for your last meal."

"That's a happy thought," said Hawker. "I feel better already."

"And maybe we can share a cell!"

"Gee, what fun."

"I've always wanted to learn how to play the harmonica."

"I just changed my mind. I think I'm going to ask for a private cell."

"How about the accordion?"

"I'll ask for a cell in a different time zone."

Behind them, Claramae Riddock said with sarcasm that held no humor, "You two men are a real credit to law enforcement. Keep on joking. Is there anything important enough for you to be serious about?"

"I have a theory," said McCarthy, ignoring the question. "I think one of the unacknowledged side effects of birth control pills is habitual nastiness. How else can the behavior of the modern woman be explained?"

"Watch it," said Hawker wryly. "She has a gun and doesn't know how to use it."

"So?"

"The warning shot could be fatal."

A northwest wind had blown the smog away, and the December sky was clear and black and misty with stars. In the parking lot, fresh snow creaked beneath their feet, and their breath vaporized in gray plumes as they talked in the cold night. It was late; only a few cars remained in the lot.

When they got to his Corvette, Hawker faced the woman. "So what's the plan, Detective? Do you want Paul and me to follow you in, or are you going to radio for reinforcements?"

Riddock didn't smile. "Paul can drive himself. I'll ride with you."

"You trust him but you don't trust me? Keep it up, Detective, and you're really going to hurt my feelings."

"Paul grew up in Detroit; he has family here. There's not much chance he'll bolt. And if he does, we know where to find him. You're a different story, Hawker. I'll have a uniform give me a ride back to my car."

"And, once we're alone, what's to stop me from knocking you on the head and dumping you in a ditch?"

The woman reached into her purse and produced the .38. "Hawker, don't think for one minute I won't use this if you make me. Get it through your head: You're under arrest. I've taken your gun, I've read you your rights, and you're in one hell of a lot of trouble. Instead of thinking up wisecracks, I'd be concentrating on which lawyer to call."

Hawker said nothing. McCarthy jingled the car keys in his hand. "Sorry, James. This is my fault. I was dumb as hell to think we could talk some sense into Joan of Arc there."

"Don't worry about it, Paul. Maybe it's time to spread some facts before the public. And a court is the best place to do that."

As McCarthy trudged toward his car, the woman opened the passenger door of Hawker's car. When the courtesy light flashed on, Hawker had the impression that several things happened at once:

The figure of a man inside the Corvette lunged toward the woman. In that microsecond, Hawker realized he had seen the ink-black hair and pockmarked face before. It was the man with Brenda Paulie—one of Queen Faith's people.

The woman screamed, but before she had the presence of mind to fire, the man hit her hard in the face. His fist against her flesh made an ugly cracking sound, and she sprawled heavily into the slush.

The man turned immediately toward Hawker, a heavy-caliber revolver in his hand. "I'm going to make sure you don't poke your nose into business it don't belong no more," he said with a growl.

Before Hawker could react, he heard the sound of heavy footsteps behind him. Paul McCarthy called out, "Freeze! Police!" He had both hands pressed together as if he held a weapon—but he didn't. It was a bluff. The woman had taken their guns.

It was a bluff Queen Faith's man didn't fall for. Without a moment's hesitation, the man swung and fired. McCarthy's hands flew up as his legs skated out from under him. The impact of the .357 slug slammed his body into a grotesque somersault and he landed with a thud on his shoulders and neck. McCarthy groaned once and lay still. The white snow steamed and melted as blood seeped into it.

"You!" The man waved the revolver at Hawker, then motioned at a brown Plymouth parked beside Hawker's car. "Spread 'em!" The man frisked him quickly and efficiently and, for the first time, Hawker was glad he wasn't carrying his knife. The man used the .357 to give Hawker a halfhearted blow to the back. "Are you listening to me, asshole? Are you listening real good?"

Hawker nodded. "I'm all ears."

The man hit him again. "Then pick up that woman and shove her into the backseat of the Plymouth. Did you hear me?" The man kicked him in the thigh. "Move!"

Hawker bent over the woman and took her wrists in his hand. She tensed immediately, so Hawker knew she was conscious. On the pretense of bending down to check her pulse, Hawker whispered, "Whatever happens, don't open your eyes. The first time we stop, jump out of the car and run like hell—no matter what."

"Hey, what in the hell are you doing?" The man gave Hawker another kick and jerked open the car door. "Get your ass in gear! What are you, a doctor or something?" Hawker watched for an opening as he shoveled Claramae Riddock into his arms, but the man stayed a safe distance away. As Hawker shoved the woman into the backseat, the man ordered, "You drive, ace. Do just what I tell you or I'll blow your fucking ears off one at a time. Savvy?"

Hawker nodded and reached for the woman's purse. Once again the man kicked him. The vigilante stood and put his hands on his hips. He said, "You know, I'm getting real tired of your doing that. If you're trying to prove you're tough, then put down that gun and let's see how tough you really are. If not, let me get the lady's purse, and I'll do whatever you tell me to do."

The man hunched toward Hawker. He wore a red ski jacket with frayed sleeves. He was thin, a little taller than Hawker, and he had a narrow, rodentlike face. "Don't you worry your little head about the lady's purse," he sneered. "I'll take care of that *and* the lady. You just get in and drive. Got it?"

Hawker shrugged. With a last look at Paul McCarthy, who still lay motionless in the slush, Hawker slid in behind the wheel. Behind him the back door slammed, and the man barked, "Get us out of here, nice and easy. Don't play cute. No speeding, no swerving, no trying to bring the cops down on us. Go."

Hawker shifted the Plymouth into gear and backed up. As he pulled away, he saw a man and a woman come out of the restaurant. In the rearview mirror, he watched the pair stiffen as they saw McCarthy's body. The woman's hand went to her mouth and she staggered. The man took a step toward the restaurant before he reconsidered and caught the woman. From the backseat, a voice ordered, "Turn right; stay in the slow lane." Hawker did it, and he could see no more.

They drove on in silence for a few minutes. Hawker could hear the man pawing through Riddock's purse. He chuckled, saying, "Hey, who is this chick? She's got a lot of hardware in here. She's got a big automatic and a Browning Hi-Power, plus she had that little thirty-eight I got off the ground."

"I think she's an arms dealer," Hawker said dryly. "I'm not sure, though. I picked her up in the bar. She said something about just getting back from the Persian Gulf. A missile deal or something."

The man slapped him in the back of the head. "No more of your bullshit, buster! She's a fucking cop. I got her badge right here!"

"So *that's* why she arrested me."

The man was quiet for a moment, suspicious. "Hey," he said finally, "are you telling the truth? She really did arrest you?"

"Cross my heart. She thinks I killed that Hershey highway jockey back on East Jefferson."

"What?"

"That fairy director you blew away—she thinks I did it. That's why she arrested me."

The man laughed uproariously for a moment, then

64

sobered. "Hey, I wish I'd known that. I'da just let her take you in. Hell, you coulda been serving my time for me. I'd of skated, and you'da been out of the way, and everyone woulda been happy."

"No one said life was fair."

"Boy, you can say that again."

The man told Hawker to turn northwest on Highway 75. Traffic was heavy for late Wednesday night—people out doing their Christmas shopping. When the big green signs announced Pontiac was just ahead, the man ordered Hawker to cloverleaf off. They made two more lefts and a right, and soon they were on a fast two lane. Rows of suburban ranch houses, draped in red and green holiday lights, blurred by. Between some of the houses were vast tracks of flat space that reflected the sky's darkness. It took Hawker a moment to realize they were lakes. One more right turn, and they were on another two-lane road—this one desolate, badly maintained. Hawker felt a chill go through him. He had hoped the goon was taking them to Queen Faith's—at least then he could confront his killer.

The remoteness of the road told him all too clearly what was about to happen.

Behind him, there was the flare of a lighter. It flickered for several seconds. Finally the man exhaled the monoxide odor of cigarette smoke. "Hey," he said, "I just got my first good look at this dame's face. She's a knockout. Damn, why didn't you tell me?"

Hawker, trying feverishly to think of some means of escape, said nothing. He looked in the rearview mirror. He could no longer see the man's face. Then he heard the clatter of broken buttons, the rip of fabric—and he knew why.

"Shit, you ought to see the tits on this bitch. Hell, this as good as gold to me, boy. I can make some dough off this woman, cop or no cop." He gave a feral chuckle. "But first I'm going to have me a little taste of this."

Hawker was surprised the woman was able to play dumb as long as she did. It took one hell of a lot of courage and self-control. But she couldn't play dumb now. With a wildcat screech, Riddock reached out and clawed the man's face ferociously. The car swerved violently as Hawker reached back to help her—but the goon had the last say. He brought the .357 up, slapped Hawker away, then backhanded the woman twice, hard. He spit blood from his lips. "One more time," he hissed, "one more wise-guy move, and I'll blow your brains out and dump you in the ditch." He grabbed Hawker's hair and yanked his head back. "You best just keep on driving, buddy boy. You best just keep driving while I take me a little piece of this, because the moment you stop driving is the moment you die."

Hawker nodded perfunctorily and tried to tune out the woman's initial screams as the man slapped her again and began to strip the clothes off her. The vigilante's knuckles grew white on the wheel.

Think of something!

The woman's screams had become sobs as the man wrestled himself into position. "Please," she begged him. "Not this, please . . ."

Ahead, Hawker could see the starlight glimmer of another lake. He hit the bright beams. A dirt road veered gradually off the main road toward the lake. Hawker slowly increased speed and, at the same time, rolled down his window and the window on the passenger's side.

"Hey, you trying to freeze my ass off?"

"It's getting hot in here," Hawker said calmly. "You two are steaming up the windows."

The man's laugh was ugly. "I'm the only hot one back here—so far. I got me one real bad case of the hots for this little bitch."

Hawker swung gradually onto the dirt road, hoping the goon wouldn't notice. The lake was coming up, and Hawker increased speed. The snow had smoothed the ruts. There was a gradual dirt incline, and Hawker hit it going fifty.

"Hear that, woman? We got the windows steamed up!" The goon cackled in the backseat. "Maybe you never been with a man before, huh? Maybe there's a lot I could teach you if you'd just cooperate."

Holding the wheel tight on its course, Hawker called over his shoulder, "Hey, asshole!"

"What?"

"Get her to teach you how to swim first."

"What?"

"I think we're in for a touch of cool weather."

The Plymouth lifted off the incline, seemed to hold motionless in midair for a moment, then plummeted toward the quarry blackness of the lake . . .

TEN

The car tilted perilously, twisting in midair.

Behind him, there was the animal bellow of the man as he fought to lift his head off the seat and see just what in the hell was going on. His bellow mixed with the quick intake of breath and short scream of the woman. Had it not been for his seat belt, Hawker would have been thrown out of control. Instead, he was still behind the wheel when the Plymouth plunged thunderously into the lake.

With the windows open, icy water flooded through in a torrent. The water was more than just a surprise—it was shockingly cold; a numbing, bone-chilling, jaw-aching cold. The car wallowed, lifting and rolling in its own wake, then began to list sideways as it quickly filled with water.

It was sinking—and sinking fast.

The woman screamed in earnest now. Hawker shook his head groggily. Seat belt or no seat belt, something had given him a nasty blow to the head. Water was up over his thighs and he had to force his mind to work; force it to tell his numb hands and fingers what to do, step by step. The woman screamed again, and something else cracked him from behind.

It was then he realized he hadn't been hurt in the car crash. The man in the back was clubbing him.

Hawker tried to pull himself out the open window, but couldn't. He swore softly between clenched teeth—he hadn't unsnapped the seat belt. He yanked the belt free, then hauled himself through the window. The car was up to its door handles in water.

Still holding onto the car, Hawker reached back through the window. The goon and the woman were fighting each other to escape—straining to be the first to squeeze through the narrow opening before the car went down, straining to escape the nightmare horror of being trapped in a sinking prison. They both made desperate animal noises as they fought the freezing water to get over the front seat and out.

Hawker probed with his hand among the bodies until he felt the satin texture of the woman's hair. He knotted his fist in it, braced his feet against the car, then pulled steadily, steering her over the front seat and out the window.

She exited gasping and floundering, clinging to Hawker in the cold. The man, Hawker noticed, had stripped off her jacket, blouse, and bra. Her breasts were round and full and erect from the cold. Her only clothing was the dark skirt.

She was babbling and clawing at him nonsensically, her hair a stringy mess.

Hawker shook her roughly and said into her ear. "You're going to be okay. Get hold of yourself, damn it! Can you swim? Can you?" -

Her teeth were already chattering. She nodded her head. "Yes."

"Good. Let's go—and make it fast. No stopping to rest until we're out. Water this cold doesn't take long to kill you."

On the other side of the car, Hawker heard a splash and *whoof* as the man surfaced from the other window. Now it would be a race back to shore. Hawker hoped with everything he had that the man had lost his weapons. If he hadn't . . . well, they were taking a very cold swim for nothing.

With no moon, the December sky was a black swirl of stars, and the lake was darker yet, reflecting nothing. The water was like ink had the stunning texture of slush. The momentum of the car had carried them about twenty yards from shore. Hawker began to do a strong crawl stroke toward the embankment, but he left the girl behind so quickly that he stopped.

"Come on, damn it! Don't rest. Swim!"

The woman tried to reply, but all that escaped her lips was a fast series of inhalations. "Too . . . co-co-cold," she chattered finally.

Hawker reached out and yanked her toward him. "God damn it," he snapped, "you either swim or sink, lady. You'd better get tough—and get tough quick—if you plan to survive this."

Even so, Hawker threw his arm across the firm swell of her breasts and began to pull her along in an awkward sidestroke. Not far away, he could hear desperate splashing as the goon paddled toward shore.

Great, Hawker thought. If he still has a gun, he'll just wait for us and shoot us as we crawl out of the lake.

Hawker began to angle toward a more distant corner of the

quarry. It was a longer swim, but it might give them a better chance of survival.

The water was almost beyond endurance now. It was so cold that it was like being in a vat of molten metal. His skin burned and his teeth ached. Hawker felt his head growing sluggish and his muscles becoming cramped, yet he knew he had to force himself onward.

And he did. Still clinging to him, the woman made a token effort to kick and stroke. Hawker took it as a good sign. If she was willing to swim, she still had the will to live. In freezing water, you had to want to live—or you wouldn't. You didn't have a chance.

As they neared the shore, Hawker began to use his feet to explore for the bottom. But the quarry walls were abrupt, and he was within arm's length of the bank before he finally found bottom. He shoveled the woman into his arms and climbed laboriously out of the water.

A strong northwest wind was blowing, and it was like razors against Hawker's skin. He cuddled the woman to his chest, trying to warm her. "Are you okay? Hey, are you going to make it?"

The woman's teeth clattered together. "Just . . . jus-s-s-t a little sleepy—"

Hawker swung her down to the ground. He positioned her on her feet and shook her gently by the shoulders. "Hey, wake up; wake up, damn it! You're not sleepy—you're dying. It's hypothermia, and if you doze off now, baby, you'll never wake up."

The woman's eyes flipped open and she crossed her arms tightly across her breasts. "God, I'm so *cold.*"

Hawker took off his soaking jacket and wrapped it around her. "Come on, we've got to walk. We've got to go find help."

The woman stopped in midstride. She shuddered, as if she had just remembered what had transpired that evening. "Oh, James—that terrible man, he shot Paul, and he . . . he tried to—"

Hawker threw his arm around her. "I know what he tried to do, Claramae, but he didn't. Anyway, we can't think about that now. We have to get out of here before—"

"Before what?" called a voice from the darkness.

The woman pulled herself tightly against Hawker as Queen Faith's goon stepped up over the embankment. Standing above them, hands on his hips, he made a stark black silhouette against the night sky. Hawker studied the silhouette closely, looking for any sign of a weapon. For a moment, he thought his hands were empty, but then he saw the stiletto shadow of a knife.

"We have to get out of here before we all freeze to death," Hawker called back. "Not just us, friend. You too. The body isn't geared for the kind of swim we just took. We all need to get help, and we need to get help fast."

The man half slid, half fell down the embankment toward them. Hawker stepped in front of the woman. The man got to his feet, waving the knife as he said, "Real smart boy, aren't you? Played a real cute trick driving into this lake. Saved your little girlfriend from having some fun and made yourself look like a regular hero, didn't you?" Holding the stiletto like a sword, the goon lunged at Hawker. "Let's see what kind of hero you are now, asshole."

Hawker stepped out of the way of the knife and shoved the woman. "Run," he shouted at her. "Start running and don't stop until you've gotten some help. Flag down a car or go to a house—but don't stop until there is someone to take care of you."

He gave her another shove and turned just in time to see the goon charging at him again with the knife. Hawker had time only to let his feet drop from beneath him and roll his shoulder in a halfhearted body block.

Hawker's bones and muscles were so cold that the impact was nauseatingly painful. The man stumbled over him and fell face first into the brush. The vigilante dove onto the prone figure and hit him with a laborious combination of lefts and rights to the kidneys. The man swung back with his elbow, catching Hawker with a glancing blow to the nose. It sent a wave of shock through him, like the first full breath of ether, then his eyes began to water so badly he could not see. When Hawker tried to turn away, the man swung the other elbow into his face.

Hawker rolled away and got slowly to his feet. As he did, he saw that the silhouette was already upon him and the silver blade of the knife was arching downward toward his face like a meteor. The vigilante caught the man's wrist in both hands and twisted sideways. When the man bent over, Hawker kicked him once in the solar plexus, then twice in the scrotum.

The man gave a wheeze of pain and the knife dropped from his hand. Quickly Hawker released his grip and snatched the stiletto away. He folded his left arm around the goon's neck and pressed the point of the knife into his ear. Hawker whispered,

"One wrong move, Jake, and I'll shove this knife through the wall of the eardrum, into your brain. Understand?"

The man nodded anxiously. He was breathing heavily, as was Hawker. Hawker's hands and face burned as if being stabbed with needles, and his feet were numb. Even so, he was determined to get some information out of him. "Where can I find Queen Faith? How can I see her face to face?"

"Don't know," the man said, gasping. "Get all my orders over the phone."

"Over the phone?"

"He's lying!" put in an unexpected voice. It was the woman. She stood in the darkness looking very small, very pale, with her soggy skirt and Hawker's big jacket.

"I thought I told you to run, damn it!"

"I'm . . . I'm too cold to run. Besides, I couldn't leave you. I thought I might be able to help." She came a few steps closer, and Hawker could see she was carrying a grapefruit-sized rock.

"Is that how you were going to help? You were going to hit him with that?" Hawker snickered.

"It was all I could f-f-find."

"Great. Stand by. If this slob doesn't give me a straight answer pretty quick, I'll have you drop it on his foot."

"I ain't lying," the man said quickly. "I met her, sure. And I know where she keeps her girls. But I don't know where she lives."

"Then just tell me where she keeps her girls."

The man hesitated. "Hell, if I tell you that, she'll kill me."

"And I'll kill you if you don't, friend."

"You can't do that, man. That ain't right." He struggled briefly to free himself. Hawker put enough pressure on the knife so that a thin river of blood began to flow out of the goon's ear. The man held his arms out toward Claramae Riddock. "Hey, lady, talk to this guy, would you? You're a cop—tell him! I got my rights. He's violating my rights. I demand a lawyer, and tell him if he don't get that knife out of my ear, I'll file suit."

"*Shut up,*" the woman ordered in an oddly hoarse voice. "Shut your dirty mouth right now."

Hawker felt a slow anger rise in him. He heard himself say, "The guy's right, Detective Riddock. Maybe I'd better walk him back to the road and wait for help to come."

"But we'll freeze to death, James!"

"Then I'd better let him go. I have no right to hold him—"

"He shot Paul, damn it—"

"You don't know that for sure, Detective."

"And he tried to rape me."

"Did he?"

The woman took two quick steps toward him. "I know what you're doing, James. I know what you're trying to prove, but this isn't the time or the place."

The goon sensed correctly that Hawker's attention had been diverted just enough. He kicked backward, driving the heel of his shoe against Hawker's shin, then twisted away from the knife as Hawker buckled forward in pain. He then knocked Hawker's head sideways with a well-placed elbow and hit him once more with his fist.

Hawker squatted heavily on his knees. Most men would

have dropped the knife. Hawker didn't. And he had had just about enough of this character's physical abuse. With a grunt of effort that was more like a battle cry, Hawker drove himself upward, drove hard toward the man's chest cavity, the stiletto cradled in his hands.

The knife splintered through his rib cage with the same high-torque impact of a tumbling .45 slug. The man screamed, his legs kicking, his head thrown backward, as Hawker lifted him right up off the ground, twisting the knife inside him. The goon slapped weakly at Hawker's face, but it no longer mattered. The vigilante twisted and heaved with all his strength, and the killer sailed off the blade of the knife, landing with a weak cry in the black water of the lake.

Hawker felt the woman draw close to him, and the two of them stood silently as the dying man floundered desperately for several seconds before sinking into the darkness.

The woman sniffed then sobbed. "My God," she whispered. "My God, I can't believe this is happening."

"It happened," said Hawker. "Either that, or this is the coldest dream I've ever had in my life."

"You killed him."

"Yeah? I prefer to think of it as a severe violation of that particular asshole's rights."

"I feel like an absolute fool, James, after the way I acted."

Hawker squeezed her tightly against him as he looked out over the lake. At the exact point where the corpse had gone under, there were now teacup-sized bubbles erupting from the dark water. Hawker said, "That's only because you deserve to feel that way."

"There's a real deep nasty streak in you, James Hawker. But I shouldn't complain—you saved my life."

"I haven't saved anyone's life yet, lady—certainly not Paul's, and maybe not even our own. We've got to get moving." Hawker began to pull her along with him up the incline. "If you see me nodding off, give me a good swift kick in the butt, okay?"

"An hour ago, I would have given you one for free."

Hawker chuckled. "See? We have some things in common after all . . ."

ELEVEN

Three days later, Hawker pushed his way through the double doors of the intensive care unit at Henry Ford Hospital in downtown Detroit. The nurses were used to him by then, so they nodded and smiled.

Paul McCarthy lay in one of two dozen beds that fanned out along the wall. Most of the beds were in use. All were connected to a maze of tubes and wires and complex electronic monitoring equipment that beeped and hummed and buzzed.

McCarthy lay beneath a translucent oxygen tent. Plastic tubes snaked up his nose, and an I.V. siphon was taped to his left arm. His brown hair had lost its luster and his skin was white.

Hawker stared through the plastic oxygen tent for a moment, then signaled to one of the nurses.

"How's he doing, Peg?"

"Not bad, Mr. Hawker. Blood pressure's back up, vital signs are good, and he seems to be breathing easier."

"Hum."

"Oh, yeah, and he swore at the doctor today."

"Good!"

"Yep. He said to the doctor, he said, 'Get these god damn tubes outta my face and bring me some decent food if you really want to help.'"

"Hey, he might make it after all, huh?"

"That man's got the constitution of a backhoe. The doctor says the slug smashed between a couple of ribs, went right through his lung and out the other side. I don't believe it, though. I think that bullet went into his stomach and Officer McCarthy *digested* it. That's some tough man there."

The nurse was a lithe black woman with a close-cropped Afro. She had the bedside manner of a drill sergeant, but was generally regarded as one of the best intensive care nurses in Detroit. She had worked extra hours to make sure McCarthy got the best of care.

Hawker winked at her. "After we get him out of here, Peg, we're going to buy you the best dinner this town has to offer."

She giggled girlishly. "Shoot, if you want to do something nice for me, don't bother with no restaurant. You two fellows invite me over to your place, and *you* cook dinner and see to it I don't have to stand up even once. A nurse's feet take an awful beating on this floor."

Hawker smiled. "You've got it, lady. For a night, we'll make you a princess. Your slightest wish will be our command." He nodded toward McCarthy. "You think he might wake up soon, or should I come back later?"

"Since you're only allowed fifteen minutes, you'd better do what you've done the last two days."

Hawker raised his eyebrows. "And what's that?"

"Shake that man by the leg until he opens his eyes."

"You think I'd do such a thing?"

"You're damn right I do!" The nurse went off laughing and shaking her head.

The moment she was gone, Hawker gave the Detroit cop's knee a tap. "Hey, Detective McCarthy, are you in there?" He had to repeat himself several times, but finally McCarthy's eyelids lifted. It took him a moment to focus. His smile was weak—but it was a smile.

He pushed the oxygen tent aside just enough to talk. "Jee-zus, they'll let anybody in here." His voice was hoarse—the result of the tubes.

"Nothing I like better than visiting a hospital intensive care ward. What a jolly place."

"They kept me alive, didn't they?"

"They're saying it's mostly because you're such a hard guy to kill."

McCarthy laughed painfully. "So, did you have your meeting with Claramae yet?"

"Hey, you remembered. The nurse said you were so drugged up you probably wouldn't remember what happened from day to day."

"He shot me in the chest not the head, dumb shit. So how did it go? Did Little Miss Priss get down off her high horse?"

"Didn't have the meeting. She had other plans."

Actually, Riddock had spent the last two days in the

same hospital under observation. When they finally got to a phone and called the police, the detective found herself with a sticky choice—whether to tell her superiors the truth and thus expose Hawker, or to plead a temporary case of amnesia brought on by the shock of seeing McCarthy shot and the punch she'd gotten in the face. She chose amnesia, and so a visit to the hospital was unavoidable. As of yet, no one had found the sunken car or the body of her attacker, so they hadn't taken her story as anything but the truth. Hopefully, the car or the corpse wouldn't be found until the spring thaw—if ever.

"Boy, Hawk, I can't believe I brought that bitch in on it. But I knew she was going to start an investigation, so I had to do something."

"Don't worry about it, Paul. She's not so bad. And I think she'll help."

"If she doesn't, don't forget about Randolph. He'll do all the legwork you want."

"Randolph?"

"Yeah, Detective White. Most people call him Randy, but the other guys on the shift call him Randolph because of his nose. You know—like Rudolph. He likes beer."

"Ah."

"He won't be much help on the action end, but he's a hell of a guy with facts and figures and research. His name's in the book."

"Great. I'll call him tonight."

McCarthy started to say something else, but his face changed and he grabbed his chest painfully. Hawker gave him the thumbs-up sign and rearranged the oxygen tent. "That's enough for now. I'll stop back tomorrow."

McCarthy grinned his appreciation and closed his eyes. A moment later, he was asleep.

In Detroit, in December, there is no sunset. About five P.M., the wind begins to leach the color from the sun, gradually transforming it into a pale, chalky orb no warmer than a full moon. Then the smog absorbs the waning light and a nordic wind rushes in to fill the vacuum.

Then, even though it is populated by more than a million people, the city becomes a desolate maze of concrete canyons. Lights flash, cars screech, factories rumble and clank, people rush and shout and hurry with their collars pulled tight around their ears, yet the sense of desolation prevails. The wind howls from dark alleys and steam gushes from street grates as if the great creature of industry lies deep beneath the pavement, warm in its lair, waiting for the light of summer. Hawker liked the people of Detroit. They were tough and funny and streetwise. But he did not like their city in winter. There was something ominous about it, something cold, uncaring, aloof.

Amused by his own bleak thoughts, Hawker found his way through the downtown streets, then caught Lake Shore Drive to Jefferson Beach where the narrow asphalt drive twisted through snowbanks and bare trees to his rented bachelor's cottage on Lake St. Clair.

His Corvette creaked with the cold as he got out. A northwest wind made the lake roar. In an endless procession, waves lunged at the beach, spread themselves on the sand, then lunged again from the darkness.

Hawker went inside, flicking on lights. Electric heaters were built into the floorboards—but they didn't work very well. Hawker could see his breath. It was cold as hell.

He got a Tuborg from the refrigerator, reconsidered, then poured himself two fingers of Johnnie Walker Black in a heavy glass, no ice. Then he built a fire in the fireplace. There was plenty of kindling and split oak, and soon he had the whole living room illuminated by flickering, saffron light.

There was an ancient stereo system. The Fort Wayne station was giving hog and grain reports, so Hawker found a jazz station piping out heavy bass and slow, New Orleans sax. He turned it up loud and carried his drink to the bathroom where he stripped off his clothes. There was a moment of indecision then. He had yet to do his daily calisthenics and run. He looked at the drink in his hand and silently made a long and heartfelt argument for putting it all off until tomorrow. He had already had a long day. Yes, and his face and head and legs and neck and the very roots of his hair still hurt from the car wreck and his fight with the goon.

So why in the hell shouldn't he take a break? Huh? Why?

Hawker looked at the drink, thinking: You are either disciplined or you have no discipline. There is no middle ground.

That did it. He put the drink down on the counter with exaggerated calm. *Shit.*

Quickly he changed into sweat pants, heavy shirt, gloves, and running shoes. He did fifty pushups, fifty situps, then fifty more pushups. Not giving himself time to think about it, he plunged outside and ran through the darkness to the beach, punishing himself with a seven-minute-mile pace.

Surf spray soaked him, he tripped three times in the darkness (fell twice), and was chased by a Rottweiler that could have been a descendant of the Hound of the Baskervilles. After a very long life-or-death sprint, his pace slowed to a wobble.

The run was not fun.

Twenty minutes out, his lungs burned and the tears were freezing on his cheek. He had had enough.

Hawker turned and headed back—by a different route.

Clomping and stomping and blowing on his hands, he entered the bungalow and slammed the door against the wind.

From behind him, a woman's voice called out, "I was just starting to worry about you."

"What!" Startled, Hawker whirled around.

Detective Claramae Riddock sat in a chair by the fire. She wore a white turtleneck sweater, jeans, and hiking boots. Her hair was bound back in a long ponytail. In the light of the fire, her hair glowed like molten gold, the drink in her hand was brilliant amber. Standing, she became a flickering silhouette of hips and breasts and firm jaw. Hawker could see that her face was still swollen from the assault. "They let me out of the hospital," she said, her tone businesslike. But then her manner became increasingly unsure. "I went home but I . . . I just felt restless. I wanted to talk to you about some things. I called, but there was no answer and . . . I don't live far from here, so I decided to stop by."

Hawker pulled the towel from around his neck and wiped the sweat/ice off his face. "I'm glad you're feeling better."

She held up the glass. "I hope you don't mind my helping myself? The door was unlocked, so I just came in—" She seemed to see him for the first time, and her eyes grew wide. "What in the world happened to you?"

Hawker looked down. His sweat pants were not only soaking wet but ripped, and his knee was bleeding. He realized his face must be flecked with sand. "I was out running."

"You looked better the other night after almost being killed. Maybe it's because your eye wasn't so black."

"It was an exciting run." Hawker went into the kitchen and opened a beer. "I must have just missed you."

"What?"

He returned to the living room, half the beer gone. "Your call—I must have just missed it."

"Oh." She shrugged, now visibly embarrassed at having tracked him down.

Hawker smiled and gave her an understanding pat. "I'm glad you're here. I mean it." She looked at the floor when he touched her, but didn't pull away. Once again Hawker felt the stomach wrench of physical wanting for her—the desire to see the lithe, woman's body stripped naked; to wrap his hands in her soft hair and kiss the full lips. He touched her arm again, but this time she flinched ever so slightly. Hawker motioned toward the chair. "Have a seat, finish your drink while I take a shower—" And because that small bit of body language told him the visit was business, he added, "—Detective Riddock."

Hawker got another beer, then steamed himself longer than good manners allow. As he dressed himself in soft jeans and a sweater, the woman called out, "Can I make you something to eat?"

"Naw, that's okay. I'll make a sandwich later."

"Can any of this wood go on the fire?"

"I'll take care of the fire. Just relax."

Her tone was humorous. "Well, let me do something, damn it. I feel like I'm spoiling your whole evening."

"Then fix the fire."

When he came out of the bathroom, she was. Hawker sat on the throw rug beside her, his third beer in hand. "You're a great little fire tender."

She sighed, laughing. "I feel like an absolute ass."

"You mean I'm not the only one who feels that way?"

"Now you're being patronizing. You don't have to try to make me feel better. You've already saved my life. Leave me with some dignity."

"I didn't know you'd lost your dignity. If you did, it isn't because you came into my house uninvited. And it sure as hell isn't because that guy had you in the backseat. You handled yourself pretty well. You don't have anything to feel ashamed about."

She put a final log on the fire and slapped the soot off her hands. "It's not that—it's what I said to you and Paul in the restaurant that night. I was so damn sure I was right. That grand little speech I made about protecting the rights of the accused. About how criminals are just plain, simple folks who've made mistakes—God, what a naive idiot I was."

Hawker smiled. "A little naive, maybe, but not an idiot. You were right. The rights of the accused do have to be protected.

If they weren't, this country would be in one hell of a mess—just ask the people in Cuba or Poland. But protecting the rights of criminals while disregarding the rights of citizens is even worse. Unfortunately, Claramae, there are people on the streets who should be chained to a wall and fed with a stick."

The woman shuddered. "I know that now. That man who tried to kill us . . . I can still smell the stink of him on me. I feel *dirty*. He was nothing but an animal. Did you see the way he acted after he shot Paul? He thought it was funny. A big joke. He felt absolutely no regret." She leaned her shoulder against Hawker briefly, then looked up at him. "How do people get to be like that?"

Hawker shook his head. "Who knows? Maybe his parents beat him. Maybe his grandfather was a drunk. Maybe he was born on a full moon with Venus rising. Who cares? People have to be accountable for their own actions. Period. Judges who try to atone for a killer's unhappy childhood through leniency do nothing but give the killer easy excuses—and usually another chance to kill." Hawker laughed. "Why is it I always end up making speeches when I'm around you, Claramae?"

"It was a nice speech." She smiled. "And for God's sake, don't call me Claramae anymore. I hate that name. Call me Clare. That's what all my friends call me."

"No more *Ms.* Riddock?"

She laughed and sipped her drink. "Riddock isn't even my name—my real name, anyway. It's—are you ready for this?—Jones. Claramae Jones. Riddock was my husband's name. I just never got around to changing it all back after the divorce, and that's been almost a year."

Hawker held up his beer. "Here's to you, Detective Sergeant Clare Jones."

She tinked her empty glass against his bottle. "So now that we're officially friends, Hawk, I want to ask a favor."

"Sure. Name it."

When she leaned toward him, her gray eyes reflected the fire. "I want to help you on this case, Hawk. I'll take time off if I have to, but I want to help you break the people who sent that man after us. You're obviously very good at what you do, but I know my way around this town. I have some pull, and I might have access to information you might need." Her smile was almost shy. "And if you're interested and want to hear it, I even have a plan—a way to break into their slavery ring."

Hawker looked at her empty glass. "Do you want another drink?"

"Sure."

"Then I want to hear your plan."

TWELVE

When Hawker returned from the kitchen with another glass of Johnnie Walker Black, the woman was stretched out in front of the fire. The flickering light danced over the curves of her body, and there was a dreamy expression on her face. She looked like the ultimate in bachelors' bear rugs.

"Ice?"

She sat up quickly, straightening the sweater. "What? Oh, no—no ice, thank you. It's too cold out for ice."

Hawker handed her the drink and she nodded her appreciation. "So let's hear this plan of yours," he said. "I'm for anything that will put me on Queen Faith's doorstep."

Clare sipped the scotch as Hawker took a seat on the floor beside her. "Before I go into it in any depth, let me ask you what you had planned. If your idea is better, there's no sense in even discussing mine."

"My plan?" Hawker smiled. "I've been here for two and a half weeks, and my plan is still the same: Find someone involved with the organization who is willing to talk. I hope to interview Brenda Paulie again tomorrow, but they kept her so drugged up she doesn't remember much—only that Queen Faith's stronghold is a great big house someplace north of Detroit."

"That doesn't narrow it down much, does it?"

"Well," said Hawker wryly, "even if you eliminate the Arctic, you still end up with Canada and the Upper Peninsula of Michigan. If the whole investigation hinges on my searching every big house between here and Alberta, then I think we're in real trouble."

The woman pursed her lips thoughtfully. "That's not much of a plan, James. In fact, when you come right down to it, it's no plan at all."

"Hey, I didn't say it was a great plan—it just happens to be the only plan I have."

She laughed. "That male ego of yours sure does bruise easily."

Hawker didn't smile. "I guess that's the effect beautiful women have on me."

Clare looked into her glass and didn't speak for several seconds. Finally she looked up. "Thanks. That's nice to hear. After a divorce, you feel like an old and ugly . . . failure? . . . yeah, a failure. You don't see yourself as very attractive, and don't expect other people to find you attractive." She touched the left side of her face, which was still badly swollen. "And after what that guy did to me, I really feel like a blob."

"The prettiest blob in Detroit." Hawker smiled. "That swollen jaw gives you a nice, worldly look."

"Hah. You're just saying that because you have two black eyes."

"One black eye, lady."

She took his chin in her hand and turned his face into the light. Her touch was electric, and her gray eyes burned into Hawker's. Her voice was husky as she replied, "You're right, Mr. Hawker. One black eye, not two. Forgive me?"

She released his chin, and immediately the spell was broken. She moved away from him slightly, refusing to meet his eyes.

It was an awkward moment that needed covering. He tried: "So if your plan's so great, why don't you share it?"

"Well, it can't be any worse than yours."

Hawker held his hands out toward the fire, warming them. "Go ahead. I could use some advice."

It took her about fifteen minutes to outline the plan. Then she began to go into detail, answering Hawker's questions with an authority that told him she had put a lot of thought into it. Hawker had feared it would be too complicated—a deadly mistake in any kind of urban investigation. It wasn't. Hawker was impressed.

"That's it?" he asked when she was finished. "You think if we go into the pornography business, we can just sit back and wait for Queen Faith's people to get in touch with us?"

"It's worth a shot. We'll set up a real corporation—I can file the papers and make it all official. That way, if someone checks on us, it will all seem legitimate. Then we'll get a studio, cameras, the works—we have a bunch of film gear in the police warehouse; stolen stuff. I can sign a receipt for it. It doesn't even matter if it works. Then we put out the word we need actors. We'll run some ads in the local undergrounds. Sooner or later, Queen Faith is going to try to push her people our way."

"And when she does, we'll tail them right to her front door," Hawker finished.

"Right." Clare beamed at him. "What do you think?"

"I think you must be one hell of a lawyer, Detective Riddock. You've got a first-class mind. And I pity anyone in the Detroit P.D. who falls under the shadow of your internal affairs division."

"Really? You really think it will work?"

Hawker nodded. "Yeah, I really do. The only thing I don't like about it, Clare, is that you'll be putting your neck on the line again. Like I said, I'm sure you're great at what you do. But this is a different line of work altogether. You've put together a plan for a good offensive—and now that you've planned it, I think you ought to stay away from the front."

A slight chill crept into her voice. "You'll do it all by yourself?"

"Yes, I think that might be best."

"Have you wondered, James, why that man who attacked us happened to be following you? I mean, you don't think it was just bad luck, do you?"

Hawker winced slightly. "I figure they got a make on my car. I'm not sure how."

"You're not sure how? James, those people know who you are. They have to know! I'll bet they have everything but color photographs of you."

Thinking of the movie cameras he had performed in front of, Hawker winced again. He said nothing.

"No, James, you're not doing this alone," the woman said sternly. "Paul is going to be in the hospital for several weeks. Queen Faith's gang is obviously well financed and absolutely merciless—and they know what you look like. For you to do it alone would be absolute suicide. And another thing—"

"Okay, okay," Hawker cut in, laughing. "No more. I give. Uncle. We'll work together—but I give the orders, Clare. Period. You can make up the rules, but when the game starts, I call the plays. Okay?"

The woman smiled and held out her hand. Hawker took it. "You've got a deal, partner," she said.

The handshake lasted longer than most handshakes, and then it became something else; something intimate, as Hawker looked deep into the woman's eyes. Startled, she jerked her hand away as if she had touched a bare electric line. "I'd better be going," she said.

"Yeah," Hawker said quickly, "we both need to get to . . . we both need some rest." He wondered if his laugh sounded as sickly to her as it did to him.

Clare Riddock almost jumped to her feet, gathered up her coat, gloves, put her glass in the sink, and swung open the door. Their parting became a recitation of nervous clichés.

"Great seeing you, James."

"Great seeing you, Clare."

"Thanks a lot for the drink."

"Thanks a lot for coming."

"I'll call next time."

"Stop in whenever you're passing by. Glad you're feeling better."

"Glad you're feeling better too."

Her boots creaked in the snow as she disappeared into the darkness. Her car door slammed shut; the engine started. Hawker felt like his personable grin was frozen on his face. The moment he closed the door, he shook it off.

Shit. *Shit*. Double shit.

As he heard the car pull away, Hawker wondered why his hands were shaking.

He went to the refrigerator and got his fourth beer.

THIRTEEN

In the dream, a child was tapping on the wall of the cottage with a toy hammer. In the background there were bare green hills and Irish black-faced sheep in the yard. At the side of the house was an artesian well lined with stone.

The child was smiling. He had bright red hair and a tiny, half-moon scar at the corner of his right eye.

Hawker recognized the child, yet he couldn't quite make his mind acknowledge who the little boy was. There was a mental shield up, a shield that had something to do with some anticipated tragedy. An explosion—yes, that was it. An explosion and screams and a little red-haired boy too mad to cry and too horrified not to. The harder Hawker struggled to remember, the louder the child tapped with the hammer.

And then he was sitting bolt upright in bed, the cold weight of a new Walther PPK in his hand. He listened carefully, his eyes peering through the darkness into the living room of the bungalow.

Someone was knocking at the door. A soft, anxious knock, as if the person knocking really didn't want to wake anyone.

Hawker threw back the covers and slid out of bed. He was halfway to the door before he realized he was naked. Hastily he returned to the bedroom and pulled on a pair of sweat pants.

The knocking stopped when he flicked on the lights. Looking at him through a corner of the windowpane was Clare Riddock.

Hawker glanced at his Seiko Submariner watch. It was 1:17 A.M.

She had left more than two hours ago.

He swung open the door. The blast of cold air that hit him in the chest was numbing. The woman seemed to tumble in with the wind.

"Hawk, I'm so sorry to wake you—geez, what an ass I must seem like to you!"

Hunched over, she was rubbing her hands together.

"Out slumming, Detective Riddock?"

She started to say something, then shook her head in exasperation. "God, I can't believe myself sometimes!" She paced to the fireplace and tried to warm her hands over the few remaining coals. "I can be such a nerd!"

Hawker shrugged, went to the kitchen, poured Johnnie Walker into two small tumblers, and carried one to the lady. "Tell me what you did—I'd like to yell at you too."

She threw her head back and made a whispered growl of disgust. "I left here at just after eleven. All the way home I kept thinking that I wanted to—" She looked at him briefly and swung her head back toward the nonexistent fire. "I kept thinking I wanted to talk to you some more."

"Oh?"

She was very careful not to look into his eyes. "Yeah. I'm not sure we covered everything. You know. There are a lot of details to discuss."

"Oh, right," said Hawker. "Details."

"Anyway, I paced around the house for a while, then got back into my car and drove back here, hoping to catch you before you went to bed."

"And you live close, so that doesn't explain the lost hour—"

"I missed the turn, tried to stop when I shouldn't have, and went into a snowdrift. I felt like such an idiot. I promised myself I wouldn't come and get you no matter what. I kept waiting for someone to stop and offer to help. But we're pretty out of the way here. There isn't much traffic on Sunday nights, and the cars that did pass didn't offer."

"That's not so bad—"

"Wait. I'm not done. When no one stopped, I tried to get the car out myself. I put wood behind the wheels and spun the tires and rocked it—and nothing worked. Finally I shut off the engine and started to dig the snow away with one of the hubcaps. I left the headlights on so I could see." She made her little sound of anguish again. "That ran the battery down, and now the damn car won't start."

Hawker put his arm around her. She resisted for a moment, then allowed herself to be drawn to him. "Do you know why I didn't want you to leave tonight?" he said into her ear.

"Um-uh."

"It wasn't because I wanted to discuss details."

"No?"

Hawker brushed her cheek with his lips and rubbed his face against the shampoo softness of her blond hair. "No, I wanted you to stay because I'm cold and lonely, and I like you very much."

She stretched her arms up to him and Hawker kissed her full lips, feeling the warmth of her hips press through the thin cotton warm-up suit.

She took a step backward and took off her heavy jacket. There was a new glow in her gray eyes now; a glow brighter, more demanding, more feverish than he had expected. "James," she whispered, "the fire, it needs wood."

"What? The fire . . . right." He turned and added a stack of kindling and three chunks of oak in a heap. It smoldered, then began to crack and whoosh, blazing.

He turned back around to see the woman carrying a heavy blanket from the bedroom. The hiking boots added length to the long legs, and her breasts were full beneath the ski sweater. She spread the blanket on the floor and held out her hand.

"Not many people know what a klutz I really am. I've spent my whole life trying to camouflage it—the B.A. degree, the law degree, the cold businesswoman facade. They're all just disguises. Beneath the facade, I'm still a gawky, flat-chested adolescent too shy and awkward, and much too sensitive." She nuzzled him. "What? You still like me even though you know the truth?"

Hawker took her hand and pulled her to him. He kissed her softly. "I had a workout tonight that set a new klutz high in lows. We have more in common than you think."

She kissed him then, harder, her mouth slightly open, her tongue tracing the stubble of beard around his lips. Her hands caressed the nape of his neck, then slid down his bare back and came to rest where the sweat pants hung low on his hips.

She trembled as she whispered, "I haven't been with a man for a very long time, James. A very long time. Take me, please. Do whatever you want to; don't hold back . . . because I'm not going to hold back, and I want all of you. I don't want to feel ashamed because you expect me to be timid, James. Please don't expect me to be timid."

Her mouth opened completely then as Hawker kissed her. Her lips were wet and swollen, and she shuddered slightly as he stripped the sweater over her head.

Through the silk T-shirt she wore, her nipples stood erect and he could see the round shadows of the full areolas. He massaged her through the T-shirt, then stripped that away too. Her breasts hung full and heavy and firm. The nipples tapered into swollen cones, pointed slightly upward, and she groaned and hugged his head to her as he kissed them.

When his attention to her breasts brought her to such a fevered pitch that it seemed she might climax through just his touch, she stepped back and knelt before him. Hawker wrapped his fists in her golden hair and gazed down on her perfect face as she slid his sweat pants down to his ankles.

"Step out of them," she whispered, breathing heavily. "Step out of them and turn toward the firelight. I want to see you."

As Hawker turned, she opened her mouth wide and took him halfway in. Her hands on his taut buttocks, she began to move him deeply into her, then out again as Hawker groaned, his right hand still knotted in her hair, his left hand exploring the smoothness of her neck and the swell of her breasts.

After a time, he said, "You seem to enjoy that, lady."

"Um-huh."

"Keep it up for much longer, and you're going to get quite a surprise."

She slid her lips away from him long enough to smile and whisper, "Sounds delicious, James. Don't hold back; please don't hold back. I want all of you."

When Hawker could stand it no more, he forced her mouth away from him and pulled her down onto the blanket with him in front of the fire. Her hips arched as he unzipped her jeans, pulled off her boots, and stripped away the jeans. The golden firelight made the pale-blue panties appear jade green. A pale curl of pubic hair escaped on either side, and she thrust her pelvis upward to help him remove the panties.

"Yes, James, yes."

The woman's hands wound themselves in the blanket as Hawker touched his lips to the inside of her thighs. While one hand moved from breast to heavy breast, Hawker used his tongue to explore the salted, scented depths of her.

As she neared climax, Clare moaned a deep throaty growl of pleasure, then sat up quickly. Her kiss was bruising, and Hawker could see that her face, her lips, her complete muscle structure had gone completely slack with wanting.

Taking her hand, Hawker pulled her to her feet. The stereo was playing an instrumental he recognized: "Our Winter Love" by Bill Purcell. Standing, he cupped his hands around the woman's buttocks and lifted her off the floor. Hawker buried his face in her breasts, spread her slightly, and let her settle, gasping, as he slip deeply into her.

The woman quivered as he entered her, her legs wrapped around his waist, her arms wrapped around his neck, her head thrown back and long blond hair hanging down.

Hawker used his hands to slide her up and down upon the length of him. Soon she began to tremble violently as her hips pulsed and the color of her whole body flashed from white to ruby red, and she pulled her face against his, and she whispered in ecstasy, "Yes, James, yes, yes, yes, don't stop, never stop, please, please, please never stop . . ."

The woman pushed the hair back from her face and yawned. "What time is it, darling?"

"After three."

"You mean that we've been . . . we've been on this blanket for more than an hour and a half?"

Naked, Hawker reached out and put another log on the fire. A meteor of sparks flew up the chimney as he did. "An hour and forty-five minutes."

"My God, it seemed more like five minutes."

"Thanks."

She laughed. "You know I didn't mean it that way."

Hawker hugged her close to him and kissed her forehead. "I hope not. I used up more calories on you tonight then I did in my four-mile run. Got just as bruised up though, I think."

There was a Mona Lisa smile on her lips. "I told you I wasn't going to hold back. I told you it had been a long time."

"Maybe those old stories about traveling men dying of exhaustion at remote nunneries are true, huh?"

She slapped at him. "I'm hardly a nun."

"The Vatican can thank its lucky stars for that."

Hawker got up, pulled on his sweat pants against the cold, and walked across the living room. He found a tin of snuff in the drawer and took a discreet dip. The tobacco made him slightly lightheaded and gave him a little charge of energy. He found a paper cup to spit in.

"What are you doing?" Hawker asked.

Naked, the woman was collecting her clothes from the floor. Hawker realized again that he had never seen a more perfect female body in his life. She said, "I'm going to get dressed. Maybe I can borrow your car until tomorrow. I'll have a wrecker pull my car out of the drift, and I'll drive your Corvette back here—"

"You're not leaving—you're staying here; you're sleeping with me."

She looked up at him gratefully. Hawker realized she had been hoping he would ask. She dropped the clothes in a heap and took him in her arms. "Are you sure?"

"I've got no one to keep me warm. Besides, we still have 'details' to discuss."

The woman looked closely at his face. She began to trace the outline of a small half-moon scar at the corner of his eye. "I'll keep you warm," she whispered. "And tomorrow we'll go to work?"

"Tomorrow we will be makers of pornographic films. I will wear dark glasses and maybe even a wig, and you will be cold and businesslike and order people around who come to see us."

She kissed him softly. In his ear, she whispered. "You could star in a pornographic movie, James Hawker."

Laughing, he answered, "I already have, Clare. I already have."

FOURTEEN

"I hear you're looking for talent?" The boy appeared to be no older than thirteen. He had curly blond hair combed into a punkish rat's nest and an eye twitch that he couldn't quite control.

Hawker, feeling ridiculous in an expensive black wig and an open-necked shirt, nodded. "We're always looking for the right kind of talent. You're an actor?"

"Yeah, I've done some stuff. You know, some skin projects. But I have a rep, and the rep would have to okay any job I took. But this rep is good. If you need actors, she can get you all you want—and any age you want. If you're interested in me, maybe she can do the whole cast for you."

Hawker drummed his fingers on the desk. "You mean like an agent?"

"Yeah, right, a rep or agent—whatever you want to call it." The kid shifted nervously back and forth on the balls of his feet. Hawker began to understand why he wore long sleeves. The kid was in the room, but his glassy eyes were about a hundred miles west on the heroin highway.

"We usually don't have any trouble getting our own people."

The kid nodded, his head bobbing. "That's not what I hear on the street, man. The shit on the street says you want to make a flick filled with angel babies, and angel babies ain't so easy to find." The boy's head bobbed faster. "You getting a lot of twelve-year-old boys and girls reading your ads and applying for jobs? Angel babies aren't going to come hunting for you, Jake. But I guess you know that by now. From what I hear, you and your chick have been doing nothing but striking out ever since you opened this studio last week. Everyone who shows up gets turned down."

"Are you here for yourself or your agent?" Hawker reached into the desk, took a pencil—and also switched on the tape recorder. He began doodling on a notepad. "What's wrong if we just want to hire you? What's the big problem if we'd rather cast the project ourselves than turn it over to some pimp agent who's going to knock you for twenty percent and us for ten percent plus a point or two on the gross?" Hawker smiled. "Why shouldn't the actors and producers share the profits instead of making it a threesome?"

The kid began to rock faster now, distraught. "Hey, I hear what you're saying, man. It makes sense. But I got this rep, like I said. She's a heavy lady. Very, very heavy, you know? Her word's law."

"So you didn't really come here looking for a job? You came as a messenger boy."

"Came looking for work, man. You could have rolled with the idea about seeing my rep. You could have hired me in a second. I need the dough, man. The bread would truly be welcome." The kid pivoted and reached for the door.

"That's it?" said Hawker. "You're giving up that easily? Come on, we've got a film to make. We could use you—you and all your friends. We need kids, man, and we're paying fair prices."

The kid stepped into the hall. He smiled. "I hear what you're saying, man. But I got no opinion in the matter. What my rep says goes."

As the kid began to step through the door, Hawker called after him, "At least tell me how to get in touch with you. Leave a phone number or something."

The boy turned. In the same tone a teacher uses on a slow pupil, he said, "You don't get it, Jake. My rep will be in touch with you. She sent me as a gift, the easy route for you. It was a fucking *social* call, man, and you refused. She wants to supply the actors for your project. You can say yes or no, but if you say no, I feel sorry for you, man. I feel very sorry." The kid flashed a wolfish grin just before he disappeared. "If you say no, your luck turns real bad all of a sudden. Nobody should have that kind of bad luck, Jake. Not even you."

A few seconds after the kid was gone, the door to the back room of the studio opened. Clare Riddock stepped through. She clasped her hands together and shook them at Hawker. She was grinning. "They took the bait!" she exclaimed.

Hawker touched his index finger to his lips to silence her. He tiptoed to the door and looked out. The kid was gone. Hawker shut the door, laughing. "You ever see the movie where Peter Matthiessen and Peter Gimble go in search of the great white shark? I know just how they felt after waiting and waiting, and then finally seeing that big shark cruising at them from the lagoon."

Hawker took the woman in his arms and hugged her. She knocked his wig askew, and they both laughed. "You really think he works for Queen Faith?"

"Who else could it be?" insisted Hawker. "Look at it this way: We've been hanging around this stinking office for six days now, and every kook, kink, and slimeball *except* for a Queen Faith representative has been here. It's got to be her. There's no one left in Detroit."

Clare was obviously pleased her plan had worked so quickly. Her face was flushed. Hawker drew her to him and kissed her on the forehead. "You've got a first-rate mind, lady."

"We had some luck too."

Hawker threw his arm around her and they walked to the window. They had leased a cheap fourth-floor suite on a sub-urban street pocked by used car lots, bowling alleys, funeral homes, and walk-up apartments. For Hawker, the days there had been pleasant only because he had the woman to keep him company—and because there had been no further reports of kidnappings in the Detroit area.

His rescue of Brenda Paulie and the subsequent disappearance of her slavekeeper had obviously stung the organization. They had lowered their profile.

Now Hawker wanted to do more than sting the Queen Faith organization.

He wanted to destroy them, to annihilate them. More precisely, he wanted to destroy Queen Faith.

At night it was increasingly hard for him to sleep—and not because he now had a steady and demanding bed partner in Clare Riddock. He found it hard to sleep because he couldn't help speculating about who Queen Faith was, what she was, about what such a dangerously twisted woman would look like.

But he knew the time would come when all his questions would be answered. He knew the time would come when he would stare the woman in the face and pronounce judgment on her.

Could he kill her? Hawker had never killed a woman before.

But he had never met anyone like Queen Faith before.

Hawker and the woman stared down through the window as the boy came out into the street. He glanced right then left. Suddenly a black Olds with tinted windows came screaming around the corner. A door was pushed open, the boy jumped in, and the car screeched off.

"I should have thought of that," the woman said, clapping her palm to her forehead. "We should've had a tail waiting for them."

"No, a tail would have been dumb. If they spotted it, we'd be marked as cops right off. We wouldn't have been able to get close again. Let's just stick with your plan, Clare. We'll keep giving them rope until they hang themselves. It may take awhile, but I think we'd better let them come to us."

It didn't take nearly as long as Hawker'd thought.

FIFTEEN

At five P.M. they locked the doors of the film studio, which Clare had whimsically incorporated as *Double Exposure*, and rode the elevator to the ground floor.

The woman was talking about where they might have dinner. The food at The Three Sisters was unbeatable, but neither of them wanted to go there because of the memories it would bring to mind.

As they walked out onto the street and turned toward the parking lot, the woman was saying, "I could cook. We could buy some steaks—or maybe some lobster. We could go to your place, build a nice fire, and eat there."

"I don't care where we eat just so long as I can take off this god damn wig, get out of these pimp clothes, and go for a run."

She laughed. "It's not a 'wig,' James, dear; it's a toupee—didn't you listen to the sweet fellow who sold it to you? Besides, it looks perfectly natural."

"It feels like a ball cap made out of Brillo pads."

"Black hair is very becoming on you, darling. I especially like the gold chains around your neck. Quite macho."

Hawker leered at her. "Being macho has nothing to do with gold chains and a bushy head of hair—as I will show you when we get home."

"Promises, promises."

Hawker took her arm as they turned down the alley into the parking lot. The sun, a pale swath behind the December clouds, was already dropping beyond the tallest skyscrapers. It was dusk in the city: cold, gloomy, fast becoming nightfall. They had come in separate cars. She had come in her Toyota because, with its hatchback, it was easier to bring another of the movie props they had been gradually collecting—the latest a cumbersome suspension mike that was said to have been used in a local production of *The Music Man*. That it didn't work made no difference. Hawker had driven his Corvette because he'd had a lunch appointment with McCarthy's friend, Detective Randolph White.

It had been a productive meeting. White was all McCarthy'd said he was—a facts-and-figures man who seemed more at home behind a desk than he would leading a big-league bust. Hawker asked him to use the computers in conjunction with NCIC to get a list of all the local porno producers who had been arrested in the last few years.

"From those names," Hawker told him, "see how many women you come up with. I'm interested in real names, aliases, anything that can put me on the track. These porno people put a lot of stock in a name. It's one of those adolescent obsessions that they don't seem to outgrow—maybe because most of them still function on an adolescent level. I'm willing to bet the name 'Queen Faith' is just one in a long line of stage names for a very tough, very twisted woman. It's just too unlikely that she got into the business without working her way up through the ranks first."

White agreed and promised to do everything he could to sniff out a few leads for Hawker.

So it had been a good day, a productive day in what was by now a coldly calculated hunt for the woman who had brought so much terror to so many other women. They had had luck. Now it was up to Hawker, up to the vigilante ex-cop to plan their assault so carefully, so efficiently that, when he was finished, the kidnap/porno ring would be nothing but a seared scar, smoldering in the memories of the few who lived through it.

The hardest thing would be to lose the woman, to cut her out of the picture the moment he had a sure fix on Queen Faith's location.

There was no way he was going to let her risk her life on some midnight assault.

For now, though, he had to let her play along. There was no harm in it. She seemed happy and (as Hawker grudgingly admitted to himself) he was happy—really happy—for the first time in a very long while.

Clare held out the keys. "Would you mind unlocking the doors for me, Hawk? It would not only be chivalrous, but it would give my freezing little fingers a chance to warm themselves."

"I thought slavery went out with Lincoln, lady."

The woman waggled her eyebrows. "No, it supposedly went out with the feminist movement. But it was all really just a trick—and you silly men fell for it."

Hawker reached out for the keys . . . and was momentarily confused as the expression on the woman's face changed. Her eyes grew wide, and her mouth contorted as if to scream.

The vigilante wasn't confused for long.

Someone shoved him from behind, almost knocking the woman and him to the ground. He whirled around to see that three men had been waiting for them behind another car. They looked like members of a motorcycle gang. Their hair was long and greasy, and they wore leather James Dean jackets. Two of them were taller and heavier than Hawker. But it was the smallest of them who did the talking.

"You the pair that wants to make that porno movie?" the man asked without preamble. He had bad teeth and his brown hair hung in braids down his neck. The name "Fritz" was sewn in white script above the left pocket of his jacket.

Hawker stepped in front of the woman. As he did, he gave her a reassuring pat on the hip. "Yeah," he said. "We're the ones. And if you three want a screen test, you're going about it all wrong."

Fritz's grin broadened. He turned toward his friends as if to poll their reactions, then hit Hawker so quickly with a backhand that the vigilante didn't even have time to react. "Let's not be a smart ass, okay, buddy?"

Hawker regained his balance and wiped the blood from his nose. His eyes had become cold blue orbs. He said nothing.

The man laughed. "Pretty boy here doesn't like being slapped, does he, boys? Pretty boy is getting real mad, isn't he? I bet pretty boy is afraid we're going to take his sexy little lady, huh?" The smile vanished from the man's face and he pointed his finger at Hawker. "If you want to keep that big-titted bitch, asshole, you'd better listen to every word I say. We hear you want to make yourself a movie. Well, that's real nice. The people we work for make movies too. But they also rent actors. That's the way they make money, understand? They rent actors to other moviemakers." The man paused and reached beneath his jacket. He brought out a wicked set of brass knuckles and slid them on over his gloved hands. He said, "When these movie people rent our actors, everyone is happy. The people I work for get paid; the moviemakers get paid; and the actors—" He turned and grinned at his two big friends. "—get to gang bang each other in front of a camera and act like big-shot stars afterward." Fritz looked at the brass knuckles then looked at Hawker. "You get my meaning, asshole?"

Hawker exhaled softly. "Clear as a bell."

"Good. Good! That's good, isn't it, fellas? Pretty boy understands what I'm saying. And does that mean you want to hire our actors, pretty boy?"

"Maybe. We need actors. I guess we're willing to meet with your people and discuss it."

The biker's sarcasm was thick. "Ain't that nice, boys? He's willing to discuss it with some of our people."

"Real big of him, Fritz." One of the bigger hoods chuckled.

"A regular white guy," said the other.

Fritz jutted his jaw out toward Hawker. "Let's discuss it right now, asshole."

Hawker shook his head. "I don't talk business with lackeys. It's a waste of time. You'll forget everything I say, and I won't be able to understand anything you say."

The biker's face flushed with anger. This time, instead of slapping Hawker, he reached out and tried to grab the woman. Hawker saw what he wanted to do, and, at the very last moment, he reached up and caught the man's hand in his own big right fist. Glaring into the biker's eyes, Hawker said, "You know, the two of us would get along a whole lot better if you knocked off the rough stuff."

"Get your fucking hand off me, asshole," the biker hissed.

Hawker could feel anger moving through him like a cold light. He said, "Touching that woman is one of the bigger mistakes you could make today, sport. I'd hate to have to shove those knuckle dusters up your bunghole." Hawker gave the biker's hand a numbing squeeze, then flung it away. "If you want to talk business, let's talk business. But let's knock off the *West Side Story* routine, huh?"

With a bellow of rage, the biker clubbed at Hawker with the brass knuckles. Remembering that the woman was behind him, the vigilante deflected the brunt of the blow with his upper arm, caught Fritz by the sleeve of the jacket, and wrestled him away. Hawker expected the biker to use streetfighter tactics. He wasn't disappointed.

With his right arm locked beneath Hawker's elbow, Fritz began to aim savage kicks at Hawker's groin, bellowing with every attempt.

"Need some help, Fritz?" one of his gang called out. There was a merry ring to his voice. They were having fun. Their leader would kick the shit out of the porno producer and then all three of them would have fun with the lady. Hawker knew exactly what they would do if he lost, and so he was relieved when the biker wheezed back, "I'm gonna kill this son of a bitch. I'll wring his head off with my hands!"

Hawker managed to block most of the kicks, but one got in just enough to start the sweat flowing and his eyes watering. He buckled over instinctively, and Fritz dug the brass knuckles into the vigilante's stomach, then clubbed him behind the head with his left fist.

Hawker fell face first into the slush. There was a gauzy, starlight sensation from the blow on the head and the vomit was rising in his throat, but he couldn't let himself acknowledge either. He was too busy rolling away from the biker's boot heel as he tried to smash Hawker's face in. The biker missed narrowly in four successive kicks before Hawker suddenly reversed his roll, knocking Fritz's legs out from under him.

He should have gone for the Walther holstered beneath his coat. But in the minisecond in which he made the decision, he decided the other two hoods were no doubt armed and, for all he knew, they had already drawn. He decided it was best to slug it out and hope the other two were still willing to negotiate a deal, and thereby lead him to Queen Faith.

When the biker came down on top of him, Hawker did a variation of a wrestler's sit-out and spun away. The greaser was quick to his feet, but Hawker was quicker. He buried his right hand in the man's solar plexus, then cracked his nose open with a left hand that came from the asphalt. Fritz back-pedaled and fell against the Toyota, nearly out on his feet. But Hawker wasn't about to let it end that quickly. He braced the biker up, gauged the distance, then swung backward with his left elbow. The impact made an ugly grating sound, the sound of bone being crushed.

"That's enough!"

Breathing heavily, Hawker turned to see the two hoods just drawing their weapons. One had a long-barreled Smith & Wesson .38; the other, some kind of esoteric automatic—a 9mm probably, brand unknown. Both were aimed at his chest.

His stomach still cramping, Hawker shook the pain out of his right hand. He tried to give the woman a reassuring nod. It didn't seem to help. She stood just to the right of the two big bikers. Her face was white and she sagged against a neighboring car. Hawker looked at the greaser on the ground, then at his two friends. "I'm still willing to talk," he said.

The biggest of the two shook his head. He had a massive face covered with a greasy black beard. Imprinted on the pocket of the leather jacket was a screaming skull wearing a halo. The biker's meaty right hand all but dwarfed the big Smith & Wesson. He said, "You had your chance to negotiate, slick. But you had to be a tough guy. I don't like tough guys. I make it my business to kick their ass."

"Look, all we want to do is make a movie," Hawker cut in irritably. "If the people you work for have talent for hire, we're interested. But it's our project; we're not going to take orders, from you or anybody else. Why don't you load your friend in the car and trot on back to your boss lady and tell her that?"

There was something almost obscene about the big man's toothless grin. "Oh, we're going back to the boss lady. But you ain't never going to get no chance to see her. Not alive, anyway. Your movie company just mysteriously closed down, mister. And you and your lady friend just mysteriously disappeared." He swung his head at his companion. "Bobby! Load Fritz into the back, then put the chick in. Tie her hands with something. Shit, use your handkerchief or your belt—don't be asking me to do your thinking."

Hawker stood helplessly as the unconscious biker and then Clare were both piled into the backseat of an aging, slush-streaked white T-Bird. The woman tried to fight just as Bobby got her to the door. She looked at Hawker and yelled in a voice that sounded pitifully like a frightened girl-child's, "James, do something. Don't let them take me, James. Oh, *please* do something. I can't bear for this to happen again."

Hawker's mind was scanning so frantically for an idea— any idea—that he didn't answer.

The big man used the gun to wave his partner into the car. "Start her up, Bobby," he said, keeping a careful eye on Hawker. "We're going to leave pretty boy belly down in the snow. He's just a little too good with those fists of his for us to trust him with us."

"Lot of traffic now," Bobby said nervously, climbing into the car. "We kill him, we don't have much hope of a fast getaway."

"Just start the fucking car!"

The big man opened the passenger door and put one foot in. When the engine was roaring, he raised the gun at Hawker's face. "Have a nice trip—*asshole.*"

Hawker'd anticipated the deadly fire and dove behind the Toyota just as the gun exploded. The T-Bird's tires struggled for purchase as Bobby floored it in reverse, then slammed it into drive. The big man was still leaning out the window, his gun swinging back and forth in search of another shot.

Hawker drew out the stodgy Walther. He pushed his head up over the roof of the Toyota, ready to fire—but didn't. Clare's face was pressed against the window like a little girl's filled with homesickness. He didn't want to take even the slightest chance of hitting her.

The big biker had no such reluctance. He snapped off two quick shots that peeled the paint off the Toyota as Hawker once again dove to the ground.

The T-Bird's engine screamed as its tires sluiced ice and dirt into a pinwheel trajectory before they finally touched asphalt, gained traction, then fishtailed out of the parking lot and onto the street.

Hawker jumped to his feet. He didn't notice that he was soaked with slush, or that his nose was bleeding.

He holstered the Walther, drew out his keys, and threw open the door of his midnight-blue Corvette Stingray . . .

SIXTEEN

Hawker downshifted and skidded into the street. It was rush hour, going-home time for a quarter million tired, hungry workers—and they all seemed to own cars.

But the only four cars Hawker was interested in were the ones he could see between him and the white T-Bird.

A cavern dusk had descended upon the city, a palpable absence of light and heat and color interrupted only by the penetrating reds of brakelights and the wind-random pitch and yaw of plastic Santas affixed to light standards.

Hawker hung on the bumper of the car in front of him, looking for an opening to pass.

Ahead, the T-Bird turned east on 7-Mile Road, and Hawker fishtailed after them. Traffic was faster there, but no less heavy. McDonald's, Arby's, Burger King, Pizza Hut blurred by, molded tributes to plasticism and bad food. A steady line of headlights streamed by in the opposite lane, so Hawker was surprised when the T-Bird shot into the passing lane and jumped four more cars ahead, running two approaching automobiles off the road. Their horns screamed, and a hubcap wheeled crazily down the middle of the road—someone had hit the curb.

Without hesitation, Hawker steered the Corvette into the temporary vacuum, downshifted into second, and touched the accelerator. The 427-cubic-inch engine paused for a microsecond then vised Hawker's head to the seat with a awesome acquisition of G-forces.

He dropped the Corvette back into traffic just as a cement truck blared by.

Once again he was four cars behind the T-Bird.

For a long time, the rush of traffic made it impossible to get any closer. But then the T-Bird veered north onto the Southfield Freeway—a fast multilane highway, and Hawker knew he was in for a race.

On the access ramp, the T-Bird began a long acceleration that did not end even when it melted into the heavy traffic. Hawker tapped the steering wheel nervously while the cars ahead of him seemed to putter past the runway. Then, when his chance came, he whipped the Corvette right and jammed the accelerator to the floor.

The Corvette seemed to squat lower over the road as the back tires screamed, then the car gave a shudder, and suddenly Hawker was being propelled toward the concourse as if in a rocket sled.

Holding the wheel at the ten-and-two position, Hawker drifted the long runway curve, then burst into the line of traffic. He glanced down at the speedometer. Despite the 55-mph speed limit, Detroit freeway traffic usually moved along at 70.

The Corvette was already showing 110 mph, and the engine was still winding, far from top end.

He backed off a little, holding it at that speed. The road was a salt-stained gray, and the Corvette was absorbing it at a tremendous rate. The cars he passed seemed to be standing still. Ahead he could see the white T-Bird dodging in and out of traffic like a halfback, but still trying to stick close to the right lane.

That made Hawker suspicious, so he too began to maneuver back across the highway—and just in time too.

At the last moment, the T-Bird veered along an exit ramp, and Hawker had to do some inspired driving to cut behind one car, ahead of another, and follow along.

He was close enough now to see the woman's head bobbing. Then her face turned toward him, and Hawker hit his high beams. He could see her pretty shape clearly: She was saying something, motioning . . . motioning him away? Yes, she was telling him to give up his chase.

Hawker wondered if they were coaching her from inside the car. He decided they must be. He remembered the look of sheer dread on her face, remembered how she had pleaded for him to help her.

Hawker decided it was a good sign. If the bikers wanted her to wave him away, then they were undoubtedly worried about him. Also, they hadn't had the time to attack the woman sexually. It meant they would want to keep her around, that they probably would use her as a bargaining tool if Hawker was able to force them to stop.

He decided it was best to keep pressure on them until they

led him to Queen Faith's, or until he thought of a way to snatch the woman away.

Hawker pressed the accelerator and moved in tight on their bumper. They were rounding the big access curve that straightened onto 8-Mile Road, another fast highway. The T-Bird tried to increase its speed, but it fishtailed slightly, unable to match the Corvette's handling.

Abruptly, the T-Bird's brakelights flared. Hawker downshifted, but not without first slamming into the white car's bumper. He fought the steering wheel until he had the Corvette under control, then was surprised to see the T-Bird brake again.

This time Hawker accelerated instead of downshifting and passed the T-Bird on the berm, throwing ice and rocks into the brilliant wedge of the car's lights. The T-Bird tried to pass, but Hawker blocked it, trying to force them to stop before they got onto 8-Mile Road, swerving every time they swerved, gradually slowing to a crawl.

For a time, it seemed as if it would work, as if it were the smart thing to do. The T-Bird just didn't have the mobility to get around the Corvette. But they had something else. The window shattered behind him, and it took the vigilante a moment to realize they were shooting at him. Hawker took out the Walther and placed it in the bucket seat beside him as he began a series of S-skids. The entrance ramp was close now, so Hawker knew he had to do something to stop them, and do it quickly. Then it suddenly came to him. It might work—if he was lucky.

He slowed a little and let the T-Bird start to pass. He felt the Corvette's fiberglass body shudder as more slugs cracked through it. When the car was halfway past, Hawker turned sharply. His port fender collided with the T-Bird, and the white car wheeled crazily up the side on a snowy incline, then came to a stop.

Keeping the body of his car between him and the bikers, Hawker jumped out of the Stingray, the Walther ready. If they wanted a shootout, he would give it to them—as long as they kept the girl out of the way. And they probably would. After all, she was valuable property.

"You ready to talk business now?" Hawker called over the roof of his car.

"I was just getting ready to ask you the same thing," the big biker called back. "Fritz is dead. I think the cops call that murder."

"Dead? You shot him by mistake, right?"

"Naw, naw—he just stopped breathing. Scared the hell out of your girlfriend—I think she was getting real fond of him. You hit him too hard, man. You hit him way too hard. You're a killer, and I'm a witness. But I tell you what: If you come along with us nice and quiet, I won't say one word to the cops. Promise. How about it?"

"Don't do it, Hawk!" Clare yelled. "They want to kill you; they want to—"

Hawker heard a cracking sound, a momentary silence, then the woman's gasp of pain. They had slapped her down.

"I'd rather just stay right here and wait for you to show yourselves," Hawker called back. He held the Walther ready, eager to use it. "Sooner or later you have to move. And when you do, I'll see if we can't open up negotiations again."

"Hey—what the hell are you, a cop or something?" the man yelled back. Hawker almost smiled at the nervousness in the big biker's voice.

"I'm just an honest skin-flick maker who doesn't like to get shit on."

"We still got the woman, buddy. Don't forget that—we got the woman."

"And if you so much as touch her again, I'll see to it the both of you spend eternity saying grace through your assholes . . . Understand? *Understand?*"

There was no answer.

The white fluorescence of the freeway bled across the snow patches and rank weed, giving Hawker enough light to see the T-Bird plainly. He held the Walther in both hands, waiting for a shot. But no one moved. Hawker glanced nervously over his shoulder. He was glad the ramp didn't get more traffic. Sooner or later though, a car was bound to come shooting down the ramp. And, if the car stopped, the bikers would just be able to add to their list of hostages.

Hawker decided to act.

It wasn't much of an act.

Yelling "Run, Clare, run!" he sprinted across the open ground between the two cars, dove, rolled, and came up ready to shoot the two men dead. He caught himself just in time. They sat behind the car with Clare Riddock between them, both of their handguns pressed to her temple.

There was no way she could have run. Had Hawker shot either of them, they would have immediately killed the girl.

The big biker laughed. "You catch on quick, pretty boy.

Now just rid yourself of that piece before we do serious damage to your ladyfriend. No, no, don't even let yourself think what you're thinking. Sure, you might be able to get one of us. But the minute you try anything cute, this little bitch's brain gets reamed, and then the one of us left shoots you." As Hawker slowly let the Walther roll off his finger and fall to the ground, the biker added, "I don't mind an honest bluff, but I sure as hell don't like a man who ain't got the balls to see it backed up." He stood up and walked quickly toward Hawker. The vigilante saw the kick coming, but there was little he could do. He dropped to his knees, his groin throbbing with pain.

"You killed Fritz!" the biker screamed, kicking Hawker in the head. "You killed Fritz—and for what? For what? *Nothing!*"

Hawker tried to shield his head. He heard the woman scream . . . and then he was in the gauzy space of a psychedelic tunnel, falling, falling, spinning, spinning like Alice on her trip to . . .

SEVENTEEN

Hawker awoke in darkness. Complete, all-encompassing, total darkness.

He stirred, not sure what had happened, not sure where he was. His head hurt, his neck hurt, his stomach was in knots. He gave careful thought to the possibility he had a hall-of-fame hangover. It must have been some party. He could remember nothing.

Then it began to come back to him. A chunk and a swath at a time. They had beaten him. They had taken the woman. Now where in the hell was he?

Hawker sat up experimentally and moved his legs. He was on a bed . . . no, a cot. Creaky springs and the smell of mildew. His feet found the floor, and only then did he realize they had taken his shoes. He still had his pants on, though, and his shirt, but that was all. His Randall knife was gone, and so was the shoulder holster that had held the Walther, and so, thankfully, was the idiotic wig. They had even taken his watch.

Hawker touched his face. It was caked with something.

Dried blood. He snorted, hacked, and spit into the darkness and found he could breathe through his nose again.

Finally he stood, fighting an unexpected wave of vertigo. The floor was wooden, cold, and the darkness was still total. It was as if someone had sewn his eyelids shut, then taped patches over them.

Holding his hands out like a blind man, he began to explore the room. When he found the wall, he followed it. It was a small room with bare walls. No pictures, no light switches, no windows, nothing. Finally he arrived at the cot again. He couldn't quite believe it—he had found no door.

No door?

He made two more trips around the room and still found no knob, no seal that indicated the presence of an exit. How in the hell had he gotten in? More important, how in the hell would he get out?

Frustrated, he sat on the cot and forced himself to consider the possibilities. He came up with four: There could be a sliding wall; there could be a door in the ceiling; there could be a door in the floor. The fourth possibility was that they had built the room around him. He discarded it, amused at his own meticulousness.

With each wall in turn, he tried with all his strength to force some movement. His shoulders creaked, but the walls didn't budge. He rested for a time, then climbed up on the cot and reached above him—the ceiling was still too high to touch. He tried jumping and still did not touch it. He decided he could make the cot into a kind of ladder if necessary, but he would save that until he finished his search of the floor.

Crawling on his belly, Hawker used his fingertips to explore the cracks in the floor, inch by inch, foot by foot. When he got to that section of floor under the cot, he shoved the cot roughly out of the way.

And that's where he found the door, what had to be the door. He could not tell exactly how it was cut into the floor, but there was a heavy metal latch that, he assumed, could be maneuvered from either side.

Hawker expected it to be locked—and it was.

He pried at it with his hands until he felt the skin break and the warm trickle of his own blood. Then he tried using his heels, kicking at the latch. In the darkness, though, he couldn't hit it squarely, and only succeeded in scraping most of the skin off his ankles.

Finally he threw the mattress off the wire cot and began to take the cot apart piece by piece. The two metal braces weren't quite right—too soft. At last, he snapped off one of the cot's leg posts and jammed it under the latch bolt. Using the post as a fulcrum, Hawker put all his weight into snapping the bolt away . . . and suddenly he heard a snap and clatter from beneath the floor.

Whatever was holding the latch had broken.

Hawker dropped to his knees, pulled the bolt up, and slammed it back . . . and the whole floor seemed to give away, and once again he was falling, falling, riding headfirst down some kind of slick metal chute toward a bright white light . . .

Detective Claramae Riddock prayed for unconsciousness. Fear moved through her like an acid, and it seemed as if she could not get enough air no matter how fast she breathed.

"It won't be so bad, dearie," said an oily female voice. "In fact, you may come to enjoy it. I do hope so. I really do. It will be so much less . . . *messy* that way."

Riddock struggled once again against the leather belts that held her on the low, hard examination table. Her wrists were strapped above her head, and her legs were pulled wide, buckled to the bottom of the table that had been positioned so that her pelvis was arched, lower than her head.

The leather cut into her skin, but would not give.

The two bikers had stripped her naked. They had gawked and leered and made obscene gestures. They talked between themselves and let their hands brush her as if by accident. They had said things that made her want to gag. She thought she knew what they planned to do, and that was terrifying enough.

But she was wrong. The bikers did not rape her. They left abruptly when they finished securing her, as meekly as toy soldiers.

No, they had not raped her—but the horror of rape didn't compare to the sheer, bleak terror she now felt.

The room was large, clinical and cold. The tile on the floor had yellowed with age, and the wires to the neon light overhead had been spliced with electrical tape. In the far corner of the room, an ornate bed sat on a patch of wine-red carpet. Behind it, the old stone wall was painted white. Overhead were banks of lights and a camera on a remote track. Strangely, the small film set somehow seemed colder, more clinical than the rest of the room.

"Still nervous, dearie?" purred the deep female voice. "Oh, I know why. It's because the two of us are all alone in this big room, and I'm the only one still in clothes."

Clare swung her head away, then looked back in a sort of horrified fascination as the woman began to undress.

She was a grotesquely fat woman. She stood on thick ham legs wearing a tentlike kimono. She had a massive cherub face, white hair stacked in a pile atop the huge head, pale lashes, buttery white skin, and a tiny, oval mouth painted bright red from which a black cigarette dangled. When she laughed, the layers of jowl beneath her chin quivered, and when she talked, her head tilted back strangely and her eyelids fluttered as her hands spasmed up and down to add emphasis.

It was Queen Faith . . . Queen Faith, the murderess; Queen Faith, the kidnapper; Queen Faith, the scavenger that fed on lost and homeless children. For some reason, Clare Riddock had never come to terms with the idea it was a woman behind it all. She just couldn't picture a female who was twisted enough, brutal enough.

Now she could.

The obese woman stuck the cigarette in her mouth and began a bizarre strip-tease, shuffling back and forth as she untied the kimono. She stopped long enough to flip on the stereo: oboes, strings, and timpani. Humming to herself, Queen Faith slid the garment off her shoulders and let it fall to her feet. Naked, she looked as if someone had taken a flesh-colored sack and filled it with gelatin. Her breasts were long, flat tubes capped with liver-tinted nipples, and her buttocks were like massive scoops of yellowed lard. Despite her white hair color, the woman's pubic thatch was jet black, a tiny dark streak amid all the folds of white, like a scar.

Clare could look no longer, and she jerked her head away with a dolorous moan.

The smile that seemed to have been painted on the fat woman's lips vanished. The tiny mouth crinkled into a sneer. "Too *ugly* for you, little miss priss?" she said with heavy sarcasm. "Too disgusting for you to even take the trouble to look?" Her sandals clippity-clopped as she hurried toward a steel medicine cabinet. Still talking, she unlocked it. "Well, let me tell you something, you little bitch. I don't need a beautiful body because I can take all the beautiful bodies I want. Tonight I'm taking yours. That's right—yours!" Queen Faith snapped open the locks and removed a syringe, alcohol, and a tiny vial filled with a milky liquid. "And let me tell you something else, dearie: Before you leave this house, you'll be begging to have the chance to please me. Understand that? You'll be *begging*. Mark my words. You'll get down on your knees and plead for a chance to satisfy me."

Before filling the syringe, the obese woman reached beneath the cabinet and pulled out a leather garter belt into which was built a black plastic phallus.

Behind her, Clare Riddock moaned softly as the fat woman strapped the weird contraption around her hips.

"Please don't do this to me," the detective pleaded. "I'll give you money; I'll give you anything. But don't do this, for God's sake. If there is any humanity in you at all, don't do this."

Holding the syringe up to the light and tapping out the air bubbles, Queen Faith walked toward her. She spit the cigarette from her mouth, crushed it out, and grinned obscenely. "I'm going to give you something that will make it all a lot of fun, dearie. A great deal of fun. In fact, you're going to *love* it."

Queen Faith pointed the needle at the naked woman and

moved in to administer the injection. She stopped suddenly, her head cocked.

Had she heard the muted sound of a gunshot, or was it just her imagination?

She decided it was her imagination.

Once again she drew back the needle, ready to inject it into the naked girl's arm.

As Clare Riddock's mouth formed to scream, the obese woman began to laugh. More than anything else, she loved these nights with a new girl; these nights flavored with incense, with violence and the sticky, dreamy sweetness of cocaine. She delighted in these nights when, more than any other moment in her life, she dominated, she controlled. They were nights when she could force the female of the species to pleasure her.

In truth, this is why she had built her empire. This is why she had forged an organization built on fear, on drugs, on bribes and blackmail. This is what it was all for—so that she could have any beautiful woman she truly wanted. The younger, the better. The more helpless, the more desirable. The vulnerability of her women always touched her as very funny. Queen Faith continued to laugh now. She laughed until her body shook and all the rolls of fat slapped in chaotic motion . . .

EIGHTEEN

James Hawker tried to slow his descent as he plunged onward toward the speck of light.

It was not easy to do. He was in some kind of metal tube, a tube slicker than a sliding board and much steeper.

He pressed his arms out against the tube, trying to use his elbows like a toe-break on a soap-box derby car. Gradually he began to slow, but then his shirt ripped, the skin peeled off his arms, and he was falling again.

The entire trip took less than five seconds. It seemed like half an hour.

Finally the tube seemed to flatten and lift, and then Hawker was flying forward, tucking and somersaulting, his whole body braced for the shock of impact. It was not as bad as he'd expected. He whoofed into a pile of cardboard boxes and got slowly to his feet. Now he seemed to be in some kind of small rectangular cement vat. The tube that had conveyed him came down out of the bare wooden ceiling above him.

What in the hell kind of place was this, anyway? Some kind of weird funhouse?

At least he could see. Light spilled over the high walls of the vat. Hawker took survey of his injuries. His shirt and pants were torn and splotched with his own blood. His neck and back still ached from the beating he had taken. His arms were badly scraped. His hands were bruised and his bare feet were streaked with blood.

He could only guess at how his face looked—not good, judging from the puffiness and the tenderness. But he was alive. He would survive if he could find a way out.

Funny how much better he felt now that he could see. For the first time since he had awakened in the darkness, his sense of optimism returned—and his sense of anger.

First, he had to find the woman. And he had to find her fast. With his wig off, it was just a matter of time before Queen Faith's people realized who he was. Someone would connect him with the rescue of Brenda Paulie and with the disappearance of her keeper. It wouldn't take a wild jump of logic for them to assume he and the woman were cops.

And to be a cop in the hands of the Queen Faith organization was to be dead.

Hawker climbed up the stack of boxes, jumped, and caught the top edge of the vat. He pulled himself up, then rested on his belly for a moment, lying on the edge of the wall.

He was in some kind of cellar. A bare light bulb produced the light. The walls were damp, built of heavy rock. He was, indeed, in some kind of permanent vat or pool. There was another a few feet away, and a squat, powerful-looking furnace next to that. The furnace did not seem to be working, and the place smelled damp and musty. Dark corridors led off on three sides.

Hawker swung down off the wall. He wanted to get upstairs. If he was in Queen Faith's residence, upstairs seemed the mostly likely place to find Clare Riddock.

He chose a corridor at random. The cellar seemed to spread itself into wings—apparently beneath the wings of a very large, very old house. Hawker noticed that most of the storage, stacked on shelves and in corners, looked like things you might find in an out-of-date doctor's office: broken gurneys, powders and liquids in antique bottles on chipped metal shelves. Could they have somehow locked him in an abandoned hospital?

Hawker wondered as he hurried along.

The corridor he chose was darker than the room that contained the vats and the furnace. Gradually his eyes adjusted. As he rounded a corner, he began to notice a nauseating odor. The farther he moved down the hall, the stronger the miasma became. It took him a moment to recognize the smell: It was that of human excrement.

Hawker stopped, straining to listen. From somewhere, some other room in the house, he could hear the woodwind refrain of classical music. The music was muted beyond recognition. But Hawker heard something else too. He heard someone calling out, someone calling softly, almost moaning:

"Help me . . . Won't someone help me? . . . *Please* help me."

Hawker broke into a sprint. He slid around a corner in the darkest part of the corridor. There the stench was overpowering. He had to strain to see through the dusky light. The hall seemed to be built like a stable. There were five or six stalls behind the sliding doors and barred windows. Hawker stopped to listen again. The voice was silent, but now he sensed the presence of life in the darkness.

"Clare," he called. "Clare, can you hear me?"

He heard the rustle of straw and the clank of chains off to his left. He put his hands around the bars and looked in. There was just enough light to see the dim shape of someone in the corner, someone on her knees, head bent, long hair hanging in a matted tangle.

"Clare! Clare, it's me, Hawk."

A girl's voice answered mechanically, repeating a plea by rote: "Water, please. I need water. Queen Faith said we're supposed to have water any time we want, and it's not fair for you guards to torture us—" Her eyes widened. "Hey, hey—who are you? You're not one of the guards. Who are you?"

Hawker locked his fists around the bars. His eyes had adjusted to the darkness, and he could see her better now.

It wasn't Clare.

The girl might have been sixteen. She had stringy blond hair and a haggard face that clearly would have been beautiful had she been cleaned up. She wore only a soiled skirt, no blouse, and straw and dirt had matted onto her breasts. In the darkness, she looked like some pathetic creature from the Middle Ages.

Whispering, Hawker tried to calm her. "You're right, I'm not a guard. I'm a friend. I'm going to help you get out of here. But you're going to have to help me too." Hawker reached his hand through the bars. "What's your name?"

The girl stood and looked at the outstretched hand suspiciously. She took another step back. "My name is Elizabeth. Elizabeth Harrington."

Hawker recognized the name from his list of kidnap victims. He tried to remember some of the data. She was one of the dozen or so who had been snatched off the streets of the Marlow West suburb. She was a high-school girl, missing for nearly eight months now.

Even most of her family assumed she was dead.

"My name's James, Elizabeth. I'm going to help you escape. You have to trust me."

Hawker was aware of movement in the adjoining stalls now. Pale, grim, disembodied faces appeared at the bars to the left of him, to the right and behind him. Most of them were women and girls. A couple looked to be adolescent boys. They all had the same haggard, feral expression on their faces. He had seen that look before. It took him a moment to match it in his memory bank. It was the expression he had seen on the faces of exotic animals in the cheap, low-budget circuses. It was the look of the wild creature that has been captured, mistreated, ill fed, and beaten until it is totally, unthinkingly submissive.

"She'll kill us if we try to escape," one of the women said.

"Or worse," added another. "He's a crazy man. Don't listen to him. He's just going to get us all in trouble."

"I'm not crazy, and you're not going to be hurt—I promise," Hawker said loud enough for them all to hear. "But you have to help me. I can't drag you out of here."

"I'll help. I'm willing to try." Elizabeth Harrington stood just on the other side of the bars from him now. Half naked, dirty, she was a pathetic sight . . . except for the eyes. Hawker saw she had large, childlike brown eyes that now glowed with a hatred he'd never expected to see in a girl her age.

"Good," he said, smiling at her. "All I needed was one of you, Elizabeth. If you go, the rest of them will follow."

She reached up tremulously and touched his hand. "I'll go. I'll do anything you ask. Just get me out of here. Just get me home."

"I will, Elizabeth. I promise. But first, you have to tell me about this place. Where are the guards? Where do they stay? Where do they keep the weapons? Any little thing you can tell me might help."

She didn't know much, unfortunately. When they were being used in porno films, Queen Faith kept them drugged. And when they weren't being used, they were kept in this dungeon. But the girl told him what little she did know, and then the others began to help out, adding bits and pieces of information. Sometimes the male guards would sneak down without permission and haul one of the women or young boys upstairs for their own sexual entertainment. Most of Hawker's information came from the captives who had been used in this way. Because the guards couldn't afford to be seen, the girls they chose got to see more of the house than any of the others. One of the women told a weird story of how a guard had taken her through a trapdoor and down a secret passageway.

"The house is full of them," she cautioned. "Be careful. You never know when someone is watching you."

Hawker ignored her warning as the ravings of a woman who had been pushed beyond the limits of sanity.

Before he turned to go, he asked the girl, "I think a friend of mine is here somewhere. A woman. Her name is Claramae Riddock. Have you seen her? Do any of you know anything about her?"

"How long has she been missing?"

"Not long. Just tonight, I think. But I don't know for sure. They knocked me out."

The girl's eyes were steely. "They haven't brought her here, James. Not yet, anyway. Not yet." There was something in her tone that Hawker found chilling.

One of the other women verbalized the horror the girl had left unsaid. "The new girls are given very special treatment. The fat bitch entertains them. She takes them to her nasty little chamber and has her nasty fat way with them, playing that weird churchy music all the while. We've all been there, friend. All of us."

Elizabeth hugged her arms to her chest and said with emotion, "If you care anything at all about your friend, find her quick. Of all the things they've done to me, being with her was the worst; that was the most . . . degrading thing that has ever happened to me. Being alone with that animal is worse than hell, worse than death—"

"Where? What room, Elizabeth? Tell me."

"I don't *know*. One of the lower floors. Maybe even down here someplace. It's like a laboratory. They do some of the filming there."

"Do any of you know where that room is?" Hawker demanded, his voice louder than he wanted it to be.

None of them did.

"Look for her, James," the girl insisted. "Look for her and don't stop looking until you find her—"

James Hawker had already disappeared down the dark corridor.

NINETEEN

Following the vague directions given to him by the girls, Hawker found the exit door. The door was up a short bank of steps—a great wooden portal between the stone walls—and once again Hawker had the impression he was in some medieval castle.

Hawker rapped sharply at the door then stepped back into the shadows. In a few seconds, a man appeared at the small barred grate and peered through. Hawker watched him scowl. There was the rattle of keys and the door creaked open.

Hawker slid in behind the door.

The guard leaned into the darkness, his head swinging back and forth. He held a heavy-caliber revolver in his hand.

Hawker waited. He couldn't afford to make any mistakes now.

The guard took a step down, then another. He lifted the revolver up and scanned the darkness.

Hawker struck. He took the guard's wrist in his left hand and brought his right forearm crashing down on the guard's elbow.

The revolver went clinking and clanking down the steps.

The man's mouth opened to scream, but Hawker slammed his throat shut with a hard right, then followed it with a left to the kidneys.

The guard whoofed and gagged and tumbled headfirst down the stairs.

Hawker ran after him. He wanted there to be no doubt who got to the revolver first.

It was no contest.

The guard belly-slapped to the bottom, gave a groan, moved his broken right arm feebly, then lay still.

Hawker picked up the handgun. It was a .44-caliber Blackhawk, a real man-stopper. He was damn glad the guard never had an opportunity to take a shot at him. He punched out the cylinder. Even the hammer chamber had been loaded.

Hawker snapped the cylinder back into place and listened intently for the sound of men running and the harried voices that would announce the news of his escape.

But he heard nothing.

Quickly, then, he bent over the guard and checked his pockets. He was a man about Hawker's age, in his mid-thirties, and he smelled sourly of tobacco and alcohol. He carried two sets of keys: one on the chain snapped to his belt, another on an elaborate ring.

Hawker took both sets. A wedge of light spilled down the stairs from the first floor. Hawker was anxious to get back to the dungeon and release the women so he could continue his search for Clare. But it would be stupid to leave the cellar door open. It would invite investigation by any guard who happened to be passing by.

Hawker trotted up the stairs, reached for the door—and dove for cover just as a deafening shotgun blast splintered the wood above his head. Hawker peeked around the stone wall. Two men were trotting toward him. The man in the lead carried the shotgun: one of the police force's Winchester Model 97's. The other guard carried one of the small, folding-stock submachine guns—it looked like an Uzi.

Hawker ducked back behind the stone wall. If that was any sample of the firepower Queen Faith's people used, he was in trouble. As powerful as the Blackhawk was, it just couldn't compete with the fast-volume long guns.

He had to disarm them and disarm them fast. If the other guards had time to assemble, his cause would be lost . . . right along with the women locked below and the life of the woman he was growing to love, Clare Riddock.

The vigilante cocked the Ruger Blackhawk and jumped from cover, firing carefully but with speed. The noise of the .44 made his ears ring, and the heavy weapon jumped in his hands as the guard with the shotgun suddenly exploded backward as if he had been hit in midstride by a baseball bat. The guard with the Uzi lowered his weapon to hip level to fire, but was spun savagely as the top portion of his left shoulder was blown away.

The guard screamed wildly, kicking at the floor. Already suffering from shock, his face drained to a sickening gray as the blood pooled beneath him.

The other guard lay nearly still, moved only by the natural escape of gases and fluids from his body. He was dead.

Hawker looked both ways, like a kid at a dangerous intersection, then hustled out of the cellar to where the two dead men lay. It gave him his first look at the house: one of those massive, gothic, turn-of-the-century mansions built before the days of big taxes and cardboard joists. A balcony crossed the inside wall and a gargantuan crystal chandelier was suspended from the ceiling. The floors were polished wood, segmented by Oriental carpets and ornate furniture. The couches and chairs had scrolled arms and feet. The fireplace was as wide as a small room. A fire roared between brass andirons, illuminating a portrait over the mantel: an oil painting of a hugely fat woman dressed like an Old West saloon matron. The woman's expression stopped Hawker cold for a moment. The thin lips and lardish jaw were drawn into a chilling smile of contempt. Her eyes were tiny, pale, piggish. The artist had communicated a sense of loathing, a sense of disgust for his subject, and Hawker wondered if Queen Faith hadn't wanted to affect him just that way.

For it was certainly Queen Faith. It could have been no one else.

Hawker knelt over one of the corpses and retrieved the Uzi. He checked the clip. It was full. He found two spares in the dead man's pocket and took them both. He hesitated, then stooped to pick up the shotgun. He had no idea how much firepower he would need, but it was better to carry too much.

He started to stand, then hesitated. He recognized the second man. It was Bobby, one of the three greasers who had attacked them in the parking lot.

Now there was only one left alive.

Hawker pumped another round into the chamber of the big Winchester.

The night was still young . . . and he could hear the

heavy footfall of men running in the hallway above. Hawker retreated to the heavy cellar door and waited.

There were four of them. One was still trying to pull on a shirt; they had been in bed. The first three carried heavy handguns; the fourth—the big greaser who had beaten Hawker unconscious—carried another Uzi.

Putting down the 12-gauge and picking up the Uzi, Hawker watched as they reacted to the corpses. They shouted, they swore, they sprinted for the stairs.

The vigilante waited until they were halfway down, then brought the Uzi to bead. Hawker preferred the American-made Ingram submachine gun. It was much lighter and had double the cyclic rate. But he had used the little Israeli weapon before and knew that inventor Uziel Gal's Uzi had not only been an ordnance breakthrough back in the forties, but it was also dependable and lethal as hell. With his thumb, he pressed to make sure it was on full automatic. Then he opened fire.

The first two men spun and vaulted as if dismounting a trampoline. They landed on the marble steps with bone-crushing impact and tumbled the rest of the way down.

The big greaser dove bellyfirst down the steps in a desperate effort to avoid the slugs while the fourth man opened fire with his big handgun. Wood splintered beside Hawker's head, but he held fast and swung the muzzle of the Uzi in a spraying motion. The revolver flew from the man's hand as he was slammed against the staircase wall, his contorted form interrupting the uneven line of black bullet holes in the white plaster. The man's mouth opened as if to speak, but all that materialized was a frothy gush of blood.

He writhed down the wall, dead.

That left only one.

The man who had beaten Hawker was hidden near the fireplace behind a massive mahogany sideboard. Hawker punched out the empty clip and slid a fresh one in, waiting. He pushed the wooden door completely open. It made a creaking sound—a sound answered by a two-second burst of gunfire that all but severed the door.

Hidden safely within the confines of the cellarway, Hawker waited another minute, then pushed the door wide again.

The burst of fire from behind the sideboard was shorter this time, and Hawker hoped he knew why: At ten rounds per second, a thirty-two-round clip didn't last long.

He listened for the metallic clank of the empty clip hitting the floor, but heard nothing.

Hawker poked his head around the corner to see the big greaser crawling desperately toward a handgun one of the dead men had dropped. His left arm was bleeding and his swarthy face was covered with sweat.

The vigilante ex-cop stepped out carrying the Uzi in his left hand and the Winchester 12-gauge in his right. He walked calmly toward the fallen man and didn't change his cadence even when the greaser lunged for the handgun, picked it up, and got shakily to his feet. As he raised the revolver to fire, Hawker raised the Winchester and the Uzi in chorus. "Go ahead," he said, his voice deadly calm. "Take your shot. But you'd better make it good, because if you hit me anyplace but square between the eyes, I'm going to blow your head right off."

The greaser stood directly in front of the fireplace. Because the roaring flames held him in silhouette, Hawker couldn't see his eyes. But he saw the gun waver, and he heard the tremble of the man's voice. It told the vigilante all he needed to know.

"Look," the greaser said, "I've got nothing against you. I was just doing my job. I swear." He tried to laugh, but his laughter sounded like grating glass. "Hell, we'd probably be buddies if we met in a bar or someplace like that."

"Don't flatter yourself, boy."

"What I'm saying," the man went on, his voice touched with desperation, "is that you got no reason to kill me. Hell, you want Queen Faith? You want the fat bitch? She's yours. I'll tell you exactly where to find her—her and your girlfriend."

Hawker's eyes were riveted to the revolver in the man's right hand. "I'm listening," he said. "Keep talking."

"Not until you put those guns away, man. You think I'm dumb? Here, we'll both put our guns down at the same time—" He made a motion as if to discard the revolver, but Hawker was ready when the greaser's knees bent and the gun came up to fire. He squeezed the triggers of the Uzi and the 12-gauge simultaneously, and the greaser was catapulted straight back into the fireplace. He screamed hideously, but somehow found the strength to climb out again, his clothes ablaze. Hawker watched without emotion as the dying man sprinted into the heavy draperies that covered one wall and clawed at them until the curtain rods gave. The draperies fell, and they, too, burst into flame.

The fire grew brighter. It made a nauseating crackling sound.

James Hawker knew the dry wood of the walls and the floor would go next. He turned back to the cellar, running . . .

146

TWENTY

As Hawker retraced his steps through the massive cellar, something one of the women captives had said kept hammering at his brain . . . something about the music Queen Faith played when she was alone with a new girl. "Weird churchy music" was the way she had described it.

Hawker had heard music. Classical music that some might consider "churchy." He had heard it when he'd first climbed out of the vat.

Clare Riddock was there someplace. There in the cellar. Hawker felt a wave of desperation take him. He had to find her, damn it . . . and something told him he had to find her soon.

Hawker quickened his pace.

At the stable area where the captives were imprisoned, Hawker searched the wall until he found the switch to the bare overhead bulb. It threw a garish light over the cells. Hawker could see the stalls were in a kind of stone tunnelway, and the cells were covered with soiled straw and human fecal material.

It explained the odor.

"You made it!" Elizabeth Harrington called as the vigilante came sprinting down the tunnel. She and the others gripped the bars of their cells anxiously. "Did anyone hear you? How did you do it without being caught?"

"Got lucky," Hawker said cryptically. He pulled out the collection of keys and went through them until he found the longest, oldest key in the bunch.

The old lock tumbled and the girl's door swung open on the first try. The other women in the dungeon actually burst out with weak applause. Elizabeth stepped through the door and into Hawker's arms. Her eyes were shiny. "Thank you," she said, her voice choked. "Thank you so much."

Hawker held the girl away from him. Her face was grimy and bits of straw clung to her pale young breasts. "You can thank me by helping me, Elizabeth."

"Anything. Name it."

Hawker released her and began to open all the cells, door by door. Speaking to the girl, he said, "I'm going to need you to take charge, Elizabeth. It means you're going to have to give these girls and the boys orders and make them stick. I'll lead all of you outside. But, after that, I've got to get back in to take care of some unfinished business. You'll have to keep everyone together. It's December, and most of you are only half dressed. You're going to have to lead them to the nearest house for help—and I have no idea how far that is. You're going to have to find out where you are and call the cops. Also—and this is important—you must keep all these people together until a doctor can have a good look at them. Some of them are going to realize how tough it is going to be to face the world after some of the things that were done to them here. They're going to try to sneak off like nothing ever happened to them. They'll tell themselves they can go back to their old lives as long as no one else knows. You can't let them do that, Elizabeth. It'll drive them mad. There's no way they'll be able to handle it on their own. Understand?"

The girl shook her head slowly. "You know," she said, "you must be a mind reader. That's exactly what I had planned— right after I drank about a gallon of water, anyway."

Hawker hugged her briefly. "Do me a favor and talk to a doctor like a good girl. Okay?" He looked at the others. "Did all of you hear that? That's all I ask of you. That's the one way you can repay me for getting you out of here. Deal?"

Everyone nodded, too anxious to get to freedom to talk. Hawker led them quickly to the stairs to the main room of the mansion—but one look told him there was no way they could get out that way. The room was engulfed in flames, and the heat was withering.

The vigilante backtracked to the cellar where he found a coal chute. He forced it open, and suddenly it was winter again. Snow lay upon the ground and the midnight stars glimmered in the black sky.

One by one, he helped the women and boys step through. He got his first look at the outside of the mansion now: a massive four-story gothic structure built of wood. It had oculus portholes in the high gable, sloping dormers, and a black wrought-iron roof cresting. On the ground and second floors, bright orange flames flickered within the tombstone-shaped windows.

Elizabeth Harrington was the last to leave. She stopped and gave Hawker an emotional hug. "Thank you. Thank you so very much," she said. "I'm going to see you again, aren't I? I have to see you again."

"I hope so, Elizabeth. I'd like to make sure you're doing all right. Until then, though, you can do something for me."

"Anything, James. I mean that. Absolutely anything you want."

He kissed her forehead. "I want you to forget my name. Don't ask me why—it's too complicated. When you talk to the police, describe me as honestly as you can, but don't tell them my name." She started to say something, but Hawker touched his finger to his lips. "Another time, lady. I'll explain it to you some other time. Go on now. Take care of your friends. Hurry—or you'll all freeze."

Hawker didn't wait for a reply. He ducked back through the coal chute and into the cellar. Smoke boiled from the cracks in the flooring overhead, and the roar of the flames upstairs sounded like a nearby waterful.

The old house was burning like a tinderbox.

Hawker found the area of cellar that contained the vats. He stopped and strained to listen for the music. He heard nothing. The fire overhead made it harder to hear.

He made a random foray down a second corridor, then a third—and that's where he heard it: the oboe and string cant of a stereo somewhere beyond the wall.

The wall was made of wood, oddly lined and scrolled. Hawker put his ear to the wood, listening.

The music was louder.

He began to look for an opening frantically. He ran his hands all along the wall, but with no results. He tried finding a way in from another corridor, but lost the location of the room entirely.

What in the hell kind of place was this, anyway? Rooms with no doors, no windows, and sliding-board exits?

One of the women had told him the house was full of trap-doors and secret passages. He had dismissed her as emotionally disturbed.

Now he wasn't so sure.

Hawker returned to the wooden wall. He could still hear the music. He pushed on the wall and noticed it gave slightly, like a door on rails. He leaned against it with all his weight, and the door began to slide into an invisible pocket in the wall.

Hawker brought the Winchester up, ready to fire, and stepped into the big, antiseptic room. He saw the elaborate film set in the corner . . . and then he saw Clare Riddock strapped to the table. He was at her side in three long strides. She lay naked, unconscious. Hawker pressed his ear to her chest. Her heart made a feeble drum roll within her, and her skin was cold.

She was in shock, close to death.

Hurriedly Hawker unstrapped her arms, her legs, and grabbed two sheets off a metal cabinet. He spread one of the sheets over her and rolled her into his arms. He would use the other when he got her outside—if he made it outside.

"So you are the man who has been causing me so much trouble," said a raspy woman's voice.

Startled, Hawker looked up. The woman was stepping out

from behind a wooden cabinet that had been built into the wall. Her huge, piggish face was flushed and her pale hair was in disarray. One of the hamish hands protruded from the baggy sleeve of the black kimono. In it she held a sawed-off 410 shotgun with a stock customized so it was no longer than a revolver. "Yes, you are certainly the man. The auburn hair, the cold blue eyes, the description matches. You were supposed to have been killed, Mr. Hawker." She patted the shotgun. "But I guess it's like most everything else. If you want a job done right, you're better off doing it yourself."

TWENTY-ONE

She waved the weapon at him and stepped out into the room. "You're kind of upset about that girl there, aren't you, dearie?" Her grin implied all things obscene. "Kind of sweet on her, huh? You were worried about her, so you came to the rescue, came barging in like a brave white knight. No, do be honest. Don't try to deny it. I just came down from my room—it's directly above this little lounge of mine, by the way. And while I was upstairs, I saw that you had killed several of my men, and you've set my fine big house on fire in the process." She looked up at the smoke curling out of the ceiling as if to underline her accusation. The whole house seemed to creak above them. Queen Faith continued, "You're not a very good house guest, dearie. I can't trust you. So drop those two guns you're carrying and pull that big Blackhawk out of your belt. Drop them all on the floor like a good boy, or I'll blow the girlie's fucking head right off."

Hawker had no choice. He dropped the guns onto the rock floor. As the fat woman fished in her pocket and lit a cigarette,

Hawker stepped between her and Clare. As he did, he touched the woman's neck tenderly. Her skin was deathly cold. He had to get her to a hospital quickly if she was to live. He had no time to spare.

First, though, he had to get past the elephant woman. He said calmly, "It wasn't me that set your house on fire, lady. It was one of your men. That big biker. He turned out to be a regular torch."

"Yes, I bet," she said with heavy sarcasm. "And all for what? That scrawny little bitch on the table behind you? She wasn't worth a *tenth* of what you destroyed." The fat woman threw out her arms as if to embrace the house above her. "Do you have any idea where you are, you silly little man? You are in the house built by Dr. Herman W. Mudgett. Why do you look confused? You certainly know the name. No?"

She was right. It took Hawker a moment to remember the name from one of his classes in criminology. Mudgett was one of the most prolific and successful mass murderers in history. He had lived in Chicago around the turn of the century. There he conned a number of construction companies into building a mansion for him. Because various companies were used, no single contractor knew that Mudgett had included secret passages, a crematory furnace, and trapdoors that opened right over vats filled with acid so he could dispose of the bones of his victims that much more efficiently. The estimated number of people Mudgett killed ran well into the hundreds.

Mudgett was a murderer. He lived for no other reason. The house he built was designed as a torture chamber to serve his passion.

The obese woman smiled through the cigarette smoke. "Herman Mudgett was my grandfather, dearie. I'm very proud of that. Grandfather did quite well financially, you know. They never traced this Detroit house to him. He used hundreds of aliases, of course. He never even told my mother about it— just me." She allowed a bawdy wink. "Maybe it's because I really knew how to please the old man, huh? But he never got nearly the pleasure out of it I did, dearie. So he left the house to me. And I've lived here quite happily all these years, chubby Louise Mudgett, who went on to follow in her famous grandfather's footsteps as the much hated, much feared, but always respected Queen Faith."

"Charming story," Hawker said, trying to come up with some last-ditch plan, some final effort at escape. "You're as insane as he was."

The woman's face grew red. "Don't you dare say a word against me or my family!" she snapped.

"How could I have been so rude?" wondered Hawker. "But you do plan to kill us, don't you?"

"And what the fuck do you think, you meddlesome bastard? You've burned down my beautiful house, so you're god damn right I'm going to kill you. My only regret is I don't have time to make your death last a few days instead of just a few seconds."

Hawker had an idea. He took a step back toward the gurney on which lay the girl. "Then you have no reason to mind if the girl and I die together?"

"Are you trying to make me puke with that sentimental shit!" the obese woman yelled. "I don't give a tinker's damn about the two of you dying together."

Hawker shoveled his arms under the sheeted form of Clare Riddock and lifted her to his chest. "I'm just a sentimental guy," Hawker replied, putting his right foot against the gurney and shoving with all his strength.

The heavy hospital table rattled like a train as it plowed into the fat woman. She backpedaled into the wall, hitting her head and arms hard against the rock. The 410-gauge went off unexpectedly. It was pointing straight up. The fat woman had just enough time to glare into Hawker's eyes before the ceiling fell in on her.

The section of flooring had been weakened by the fire, and the shotgun blast was the final touch. Now flames and orange coals rained down on her huge form. Even as Hawker was scrambling to get Clare out of there, he saw clearly how Queen Faith's pale hair seemed to glow, then burst into bright flame. And he heard the woman's hideous screams as the kimono caught fire and she became a ponderous, running flare that banged off rock walls as the flames bubbled her pale flesh, then burst it.

Hawker had no desire to see any more. Trying to brush away the burning wood that was now coming down on them, he carried Clare to the coal chute and climbed with her outside.

Hawker remembered little of what happened then. Even weeks later, it would return only in bits and pieces. He remembered how the women he had freed now helped him place Clare Riddock on the ground; how they helped him bundle the sheets around her; how they insisted on caring for his girl until the ambulances arrived . . . and he remembered how one of the women burst suddenly into tears, and how someone was trying to keep him away, and how the paramedic who arrived tried to give him an injection to calm him after they pulled the sheet over Clare Riddock's perfect face . . .

And then he was walking, walking cold and alone through the December night, somewhere north of Detroit, he didn't know where—or even care. He saw a phone booth ahead and, magically, there was a quarter in his hand. He dialed Paul McCarthy's hospital number with exaggerated care, making more of a job of it than it was.

"Hey, Paul, it's Hawk. Just called to check in."

McCarthy, no fool, immediately picked up the odd tone in the vigilante's voice. "What's wrong, Hawk? Are you in some kind of trouble or something?"

"What kind of trouble could I be in, Paul? We busted Queen Faith good tonight. Took out all the biggies and freed all the little ones. I imagine your people have some uniforms out there now. I think your kidnapping problems are over, old buddy. All Queen Faith's people have been officially dispatched."

"By yourself, Hawk? You did all of that *alone?* My God, but how? You have to come to the hospital, Hawk. I've got to hear all about it. Why don't you and Clare come over tonight? I can bribe the nurses to let you in—"

"Clare's dead, Paul," Hawker interrupted matter-of-factly. "Funny thing is, I'm not even sure how she was killed. I got there too late, you see. I probably could have prevented it, but I just wasn't in time."

McCarthy didn't respond for several seconds. Finally he knew why Hawker's voice sounded so strange. He said softly,

"James, I know how you felt about her. I know that you loved her. I'm sorry."

Hawker said nothing. He tried to peer through the glass of the phone booth, but his eyes wouldn't focus for some reason. Everything was blurry.

McCarthy continued, "Maybe you ought to come up for a visit, James—or, hell, I'll just sign myself out for the night. It would do me good, and you need to talk to someone."

James Hawker wondered why his snort of laughter sounded so strange and sad. "Can't risk it, Paul. I've got to move fast now. I can't afford to stick around after an operation."

"But where can I get in touch with you—"

"You can't, Paul. You can't. Maybe someday I'll get in touch with you."

As the Detroit detective started to say something else, Hawker hung up the phone. He pushed open the door of the booth and stepped out into the night. He looked at the stars and then at the far-off glow of the burning mansion.

He spit into the snow.

He thought about maybe going to his place in Florida, the little ramshackle house built on stilts in the shallow water of Chokoloskee Bay. That was an idea. He could lie in the sun, fish when he wanted, drink beer and get fat and think about absolutely nothing.

James Hawker nodded as he walked aimlessly into the winter darkness. Yes, he would go to Florida. It was far too cold in Detroit this time of year . . .

ABOUT THE AUTHOR

Randy Wayne White was born in Ashland, Ohio, in 1950. Best known for his series featuring retired NSA agent Doc Ford, he has published over twenty crime fiction and nonfiction adventure books. White began writing while working as a fishing guide in Florida, where most of his books are set. His earlier writings include the Hawker series, which he published under the pen name Carl Ramm. White has received several awards for his fiction, and his novels have been featured on the *New York Times* bestseller list. He was a monthly columnist for *Outside* magazine and has contributed to several other publications, as well as lectured throughout the United States and travelled extensively. White currently lives on Pine Island in South Florida, and remains an active member of the community through his involvement with local civic affairs as well as the restaurant Doc Ford's Sanibel Rum Bar and Grill.

THE HAWKER SERIES

FROM OPEN ROAD MEDIA

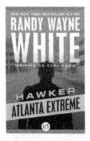

HAWKER
ATLANTA EXTREME

HAWKER
CHICAGO ASSAULT

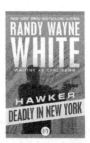

HAWKER
DEADLY IN NEW YORK

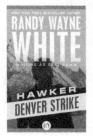

HAWKER
DENVER STRIKE

HAWKER
DETROIT COMBAT

HAWKER
FLORIDA FIREFIGHT

HAWKER
HOUSTON ATTACK

HAWKER
L.A. WARS

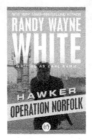

HAWKER
OPERATION NORFOLK

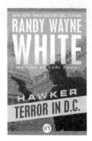

HAWKER
TERROR IN D.C.

OPEN ROAD
INTEGRATED MEDIA

INTEGRATED MEDIA

Find a full list of our authors and
titles at www.openroadmedia.com

FOLLOW US
@OpenRoadMedia

CPSIA information can be obtained at www.ICGtesting.com
Printed in the USA
BVOW08s1532200716

456257BV00003B/21/P